Fox River Valley PLD
555 Barrington Ave.
Dundee, IL 60118
www.frvpld.info Renew online or call 847-590-8706

ACT 2

by Andrew Keenan-Bolger
and Kate Wetherhead

Grosset & Dunlap
An Imprint of Penguin Random House

GROSSET & DUNLAP
Penguin Young Readers Group
An Imprint of Penguin Random House LLC

Text copyright © 2016 by Andrew Keenan-Bolger and Kate Wetherhead. Illustrations copyright
© 2016 by Penguin Random House LLC. All rights reserved. Published by Grosset & Dunlap,
an imprint of Penguin Random House LLC, 345 Hudson Street, New York, New York 10014.
GROSSET & DUNLAP is a trademark of Penguin Random House LLC. Printed in the USA.

Cover illustrations by Avner Geller and Kyle Webster.

Library of Congress Cataloging-in-Publication Data is available.

ISBN 978-0-448-47840-1   10 9 8 7 6 5 4 3 2 1

IN MEMORY OF ROGER REES,
A MOST EXQUISITE THEATER NERD.

-LOUISA-

Everything was smaller than I had expected. More compact. The hallways were narrow, the ceilings low, the rooms tiny and warm from the mirror lights. But the sweet, musty smell was the same as any theater's backstage, and I couldn't decide what was more exciting—the things that surprised me or the things that were so familiar.

If I'd been told four and a half months ago that I'd be getting a guided tour of a Broadway theater from a former Broadway star who also happened to be my new best friend, I never would have believed it. And now here I stood, as close to my dreams as I'd ever been, *still* not quite believing it.

"You okay, Lou?"

I turned to see Jack looking at me, amused. He must have known I was overwhelmed.

"Yeah," I replied, thinking how interesting my life had become since Jack Goodrich moved in down the street from me.

In November, Jack and I had finished our run of *Into the Woods* with the Shaker Heights Community Players. The critic for the *Sun Press* had given it a glowing review: "Utterly enchanting," he'd gushed. "Poignant . . . Beautifully acted and sung by a stellar cast."

"I guess you're used to getting reviewed by, like, the *New York Times*," I'd said to Jack after reading the review to him over the phone.

"Are you kidding?" Jack had replied, incredulous. "A rave is a rave. Who cares who's writing it?" I loved that he felt as proud of our show as I did.

Speaking of proud—not only did our entire seventh-grade homeroom come to see our show, but they all stood during the curtain call when Jack and I took our bows! Even Tanner Falzone, who had made Jack a target of his ridicule early in the school year, whistled through his teeth like he was at a football game.

For the week following our run, it seemed like all of Shaker Heights was talking about our production of *Into the Woods*. I felt like a mini celebrity, like when the manager at Yours Truly Restaurant recognized me.

"Oh my god, you were so good as Little Red Riding Hood!" she exclaimed as she helped the hostess seat me and my parents. "So feisty." When our entrees were cleared about an hour later, a complimentary brownie sundae was sent over.

"Woo-hoo, star treatment," my dad said, grabbing one of the three forks provided and digging into the whipped cream. "I could get used to having a famous kid."

At the dentist, the dry cleaner's, the drugstore, people would come up to me to tell me how much they loved the show.

The same thing was happening to Jack, and I asked him if that's what it was like for working actors in New York.

"Not really," he said. "There's, like, eight million people there, and most of them don't go to

Broadway shows—tourists do. So it's pretty easy to be anonymous." We laughed at how much more famous he felt in Shaker Heights, Ohio, than he ever had in New York City.

Soon enough, though, our celebrity status faded away, brownie sundaes came with a price tag, and we went back to being regular seventh-graders. Our next shot at the spotlight wouldn't be until second semester, when Mrs. Wagner, our music teacher, would be directing a production of *Guys and Dolls*. I was looking forward to it, of course, especially since the part of Adelaide was on my list of dream roles, but as far as Mrs. Wagner was concerned . . . Well, let's just say that she wasn't the greatest director. Her only objective was making sure that everyone could be seen and heard on stage at all times, which usually meant scene after scene of kids standing in a straight line, delivering their dialogue very loudly to the audience instead of to each other. She was certainly no Renee Florkowski, our *Into the Woods* director.

So sure, we had a show on the horizon, but it wasn't going to be anything like what we'd just experienced with the Shaker Heights Community Players. And it didn't really matter, anyway. By early December, everyone had other things demanding their attention, like getting ready for the holidays.

"My parents and I are going to New York for New Year's," Jack announced one night while we were at his house doing our English homework. We were supposed to be answering questions about S. E. Hinton's *The Outsiders*, a book title that was suddenly hitting a little too close to home.

"Wow," I said, trying to conceal that jealousy, "how long are you going for?"

"Five days. We're staying with my parents' friends on the Upper West Side," Jack replied casually. After all this time, it still bugged me how easy it was for him to talk about New York— like he was talking about a corner store or a gas station.

"Are you going to see any shows?" I asked, staring at a page from my book but not reading a word.

"Probably," Jack said. "I have some friends

working right now who I should go support."

Friends to support! On Broadway! I mean, I
always went with Jenny's parents to her yearly
ballet recital in Cleveland, but—no offense to
Jenny—that just didn't sound as cool.

"What are *you* doing for the break?" Jack
asked, looking up from his homework. I hesitated,
mortified to tell him.

"Um, not much. My uncle Dan and his
girlfriend, Tina, are driving up from Missouri to
visit for a couple days. She, um . . . really wants to
see the Rock and Roll Hall of Fame." Jack wasn't a
good enough actor to mask his pity. And I wasn't a
good enough actor to mask my gloom.

I spent the next couple of weeks trying not to
think about how different our winter vacations
were going to be, choosing instead to concentrate
on schoolwork and reminding myself that Uncle
Dan made really good French toast. I'd never met
Tina, but Dan had told me on the phone that she'd
really liked the movie *Chicago*, so we'd "have lots
to talk about" when they got to town. I wasn't
convinced.

For the most part, Jack did a good job of not
talking too much about his upcoming trip, probably

sensing that it was a painful subject for me.

That is, until one day when we were riding the bus home from school and his cell phone chimed with a new text message. As he read the message, he let out a slight gasp and said, "I can't believe it—my mom just got me a ticket to see *Let's Make a Toast!*"

My heart sank. Jack and I had been obsessing over that show since we'd found bootleg clips of it on YouTube. It had recently opened on Broadway and starred the amazing Madeleine Zimmer, who Jack knew *personally*. I didn't want to ruin Jack's excitement, so I mustered a "That's amazing!" and tried not to burst into tears.

As the bus pulled up to our stop, he said, "Hey, do you mind if I come over to your house for a little while? Both my parents are out."

"Sure," I said, slightly dreading the thought of having to spend the afternoon with Jack pretending I wasn't sad.

But confusion replaced my dread as we entered my house to find both of our moms drinking tea in the kitchen.

"Hey, superstars," my mom said as we approached, "how was school?"

"Good," Jack said breezily, like he hadn't just totally lied to me.

"Jack?" I said suspiciously. "I thought you said your parents were out."

"They are. My dad's at work and my mom's . . . here." He raised his eyebrows at his mom, who coyly sipped her tea.

"Did you ask Mrs. Benning?" Jack asked her.

"I did."

"So I can tell Lou?"

"Go ahead," she replied, winking at my mom.

I looked from Mom to Mrs. Goodrich to Jack—all three of them now grinning at me like idiots.

"Tell me *what*?" I demanded, my heart beating fast.

Jack kept grinning as he spoke.

"So . . . remember that text message I got on the bus?"

"About getting a ticket to *Let's Make a Toast!*?"

"Well, that was only *half*-true. My mom actually got *two* tickets." I felt a lump rise in my throat as I realized what he was saying.

"Do you mean . . . ?" I asked, trying not to get weepy.

Jack beamed at me, proud of his trick.

"Yeah—the other ticket is yours. Wanna come to New York with us?"

"Hey, Earth to Lou."

Jack's hand waved in front of my face, snapping me back to reality—if you could call *this* reality. A heavily tattooed man carrying a wavy auburn wig on a Styrofoam head whisked by as I turned to Jack.

"Sorry, what did you say?"

Jack laughed.

"I said, 'Is this what you pictured a Broadway backstage would look like?'"

"Oh," I said, looking around in wonder for the eight millionth time. "Sort of? I mean, not really, but maybe? I don't know," I stammered, nervously gripping my winter coat, "but it's amazing."

"The St. James Theatre actually has a larger backstage than most," Jack explained to my astonishment. *There were places that were even smaller than this?*

I watched in fascination as the actors nimbly maneuvered past us through the narrow corridor, loosening neckties and pulling bobby pins from their wigs. Only minutes ago these same people had been *onstage*, singing and dancing in front of an ecstatic crowd. The show had been better than I'd hoped, with songs that would be stuck in my head for months. Jack and I had screamed ourselves hoarse during the curtain call. Now all of the people that we'd been cheering for from afar were checking their cell phones and debating which subway lines would get them home fastest. I was feeling awestruck by every single one of them when a newly familiar voice rang out:

"All right, who let these *kids* in here?"

I turned to see Madeleine Zimmer, the star of the show, her eyes twinkling mischievously under her false eyelashes and her Crest-commercial-white teeth lined up in a perfect smile. She wore a long pink-and-red silk kimono, and when Jack jumped into her arms, he disappeared behind its floor-length sleeves.

"Maddie!" His exclamation was muffled by the fabric. "You were *incredible!*"

"Well, once I knew that *Jack Goodrich* was going to be in the audience, I upped my game," she said, releasing him. "Oh my goodness, let me look at you. You got so big!"

Jack looked down at his feet like he'd failed to notice his recent growth spurt.

"Yeah, I guess so," he said with a chuckle.

"And who's this great beauty?" Madeleine asked, gesturing toward me.

Great beauty? She's got to be kidding, I thought. *This woman looks like a supermodel, and I look like . . . well, like a starstruck twelve-year-old theater nerd with hat hair holding a huge parka.*

"This is my best friend from Ohio—Louisa Benning," answered Jack. Normally I would have offered up my nickname; here I was too shy. Jack, however, was not: "But everyone calls her Lou."

"Then Lou is what I will call you, too!" declared Madeleine, and the next thing I knew I was enveloped by those silk kimono sleeves. I almost fainted.

"Come on, I'll show you my dressing room," said Madeleine, and as she turned to lead us up a flight of stairs I started to feel like Alice in Wonderland. Except unlike Alice I felt big and small *at the same time*: big because the stairs kept getting narrower and narrower as we went up, and small because I was still just some nobody kid from Shaker Heights, Ohio. But I wasn't just some nobody, was I?

I was Jack Goodrich's best friend. He had just said it out loud to a real Broadway star, and that alone made me feel one step closer to belonging to this magical world. I felt light-headed. As we reached the top of the stairs, I grabbed the hem of Jack's coat and whispered in his ear, "I know this kind of thing is normal for you, but I am sort of freaking out right now."

"Are you okay?" he whispered back.

"Oh, yeah, it's a good kind of freak-out," I said, peering into Madeleine's dressing room. It was filled with framed photographs, colorful throw pillows, and little potted plants. I smiled, imagining what my own Broadway dressing room would look like someday.

"This might be the coolest night of my life."

-JACK-

"Come in, make yourselves comfortable," Maddie said, gesturing to a pink velvet couch wedged between a costume rack and giant humidifier. "You don't mind if I take off my wig prep, do you?"

"Nope," I said, hopping onto the embroidered cushions. Lou's eyes widened as she crept past the rack of sparkling costumes that just minutes before had twirled across the stage.

"You can touch 'em if you want, hon," Maddie said, taking a seat. She dug her painted nails into the panty-hose cap on her head, removing bobby pins like garden weeds. I watched as Lou delicately ran her fingers across the intricate beading on one of the dresses.

"Can you believe how many costume changes I have?" Maddie asked us.

"Seriously! There was one that seemed to take less than fifteen seconds," I said. "How did you do that?"

"Oh yeah, the purple into the burgundy?" Maddie asked. "You can see, everything's rigged."

I watched as Lou gently pushed aside the dresses on the rack until she came to the purple one. Up close, the glass buttons were revealed to be snaps, the lace corset hiding a zipper.

"There are two dressers waiting offstage who literally rip the purple one off me," Maddie explained, "then there's a third dresser who has the burgundy dress open on the floor. I step into it and she pulls it up around me, I stick my arms through the sleeves, she zips up the back, then practically pushes me back onstage. We call it the grape to raisin change, because of the colors."

Maddie began undoing her pin curls, spirals of tightly wound hair held in place with bobby pins.

"So what brings you back into town?" Maddie

asked, letting a blond ringlet bounce in front of her face. "Here for an audition?"

"No," I said. "Just for the holidays. Although we did *Into the Woods* last month in Shaker Heights, and when we get back we're auditioning for *Guys and Dolls.*"

"No kidding?" Maddie smiled. "At what theater? The Cleveland Playhouse?"

"Oh . . . no." I laughed kind of awkwardly. "It's just at our school."

"Right, of course." Maddie smiled. "So you're an actress, too?" she said, nodding to Lou.

"Erm, yes," Lou croaked, stepping from the costume rack and into the golden light of Maddie's dressing station. "But nothing professional like you guys."

"Well, no need to hurry," Maddie said, running her fingers through her curly blond hair. "Enjoy being a kid while you still can."

"Lou's such a good actress," I said proudly. "She was awesome as Little Red. Her comic timing was ridiculous."

Lou blushed as Maddie turned to her. "Well, sheesh! Stay in Shaker Heights as long as you'd like, honey! I don't need to start running into you at auditions, stealing my roles!" she said with a wink.

This trip to New York felt entirely different, seeing everything through Lou's eyes. After four months of feeling like an exchange student in Ohio, I finally got to be the tour guide. Even the most ordinary tasks, like riding the subway or walking through midtown, became adventures. Places like TKTS (a giant red booth selling discount theater tickets) or Shubert Alley (a walkway displaying Broadway show posters) became photo ops. Our favorite game was trying to re-create iconic show logos next to their life-size counterparts. For *Book of Mormon* I jumped in the air holding a stack of Playbills. *Wicked* had Lou whispering a secret in my ear a la Glinda and Elphaba. *Kinky Boots* was a stretch, but when viewed through squinted eyes, our contorted bodies *did* sort of look like a pair of sparkly red heels. Lou would shriek and squeeze my arm as she identified Broadway chorus girls walking down Ninth Avenue (the fake eyelashes and baseball hats hiding their wig caps were always the giveaway). As her tour guide, I made sure to point out not only landmarks but character traits that separated tourists from the real New Yorkers. *Lesson number one: Tourists always look up at the buildings, while real New Yorkers keep their eyes on the sidewalk, making sure they don't step in dog poop.*

I took her to some of my favorite places— Chelsea Market, the Tenement Museum, and the Drama Book Shop, which was packed with every play- and theater-related publication you could dream of. My parents and I helped prevent rookie mistakes, like shopping in Times Square or those pop-up Christmas villages (they sold the same stuff back in Shaker Heights and for cheaper). We steered her away from overly crowded attractions, like the Empire State Building and the Statue of Liberty. Although, Mom and Dad finally caved when Lou suggested we go ice-skating at Rockefeller Center (I'd lived here for twelve years and had never actually been). Of course once we saw how long the line was, we settled for just taking selfies in front of the giant Christmas tree.

The one event on our itinerary that made me anxious was a lunch date I'd set up with two of my

Broadway friends. This meeting felt important. After a semester playing the new kid in Lou's social circle, it was my turn to make the introductions. I prayed my city friends liked my new Ohio sidekick as much as I did.

Connor Gage and Imani Marie Johnson were two of my favorite people in the business. Imani was a Young Nala in *The Lion King* and a Lavender in *Matilda*. We had the same agent, Davina Saltzberg, who introduced us back when we first started working. Her hair was a cloud of beautiful ringlets, making it impossible to take your eyes off of her when she was onstage. Connor was the kid I took over for as Michael Banks in *Mary Poppins* (he had left to go be in *Newsies* just one block away). At age fourteen he already had four Broadway shows under his belt, and whenever he walked into an audition room, all the parents would sigh, knowing their kid was probably out of a job. He was something of a legend to me.

"Kodama?" Lou squeaked when I announced the spot I'd chosen for lunch. "What about Sardi's or Ellen's Stardust Diner? Isn't that where you

Broadway people like to hang out?"

"Lesson number thirteen," I said, rolling my eyes comically, "if you're looking for actors, check the sushi and Thai places first."

We pulled open the door to the warm midtown restaurant, which smelled like cucumber and green tea. My parents had allowed us to meet my friends on our own, which gave them a chance to catch up with some old friends from the neighborhood. I immediately spotted Imani and Connor wedged in a table in the back underneath an autographed *West Side Story* poster. Their trendy outfits told the world they were definitely not tourists. I locked eyes with them, waving as we squeezed through a labyrinth of shopping bags and puffy coats hanging off the backs of chairs. Just as we arrived at their table, Connor and Imani threw open their menus, whipping them up to shield their faces.

"Gosh, you can't go anywhere in midtown anymore," Connor muttered from behind his food-splattered menu.

"And I thought the stage door was bad," Imani added.

Lou looked over to me nervously, but a split second later a burst of laughter erupted from behind the menus.

"Jacky, long time, no see," Connor said as he tossed his menu and leaped from the table to throw a bear hug around me.

"We missed you so much," Imani said, leaning in, giving a quick kiss to my right check and then my left.

"This is my friend that I told you about," I said, placing a gloved hand on Lou's shoulder. "Her name is Louisa . . ." I waited for her nickname qualification, but when I looked over, she stood frozen, hugging the straps of her backpack.

"But everyone calls her Lou," I finished.

"Yes," Lou piped in quickly. "Everyone calls me Lou, and nice to meet you guys."

"It's nice to meet you, too," Imani said, moving over to her and repeating her double-kiss routine.

We sat down and placed our orders. Lou: the chicken tempura. Me: the deluxe sashimi combo. Our conversation drifted from upcoming jobs (Connor, in a play downtown; Imani, in a music video), to school, to New Year's plans. It didn't take long to notice how different it was talking with

ACT 2

my New York friends versus my friends back in
Shaker Heights. In the four months I'd been gone,
my city friends had started acting like adults—
ordering seaweed salads and actually using words
they'd learned from spelling tests. I'd be lying if I
said I didn't study every gesture and phrase they
used.

"So," Connor said as he folded his hands on the
table. "What have you seen this trip?"

"Oh, well, last night we saw *Let's Make a Toast!*"
I said.

"Hmm," Imani said, nodding. "What did you
think?"

"Omigosh, it was amazing!" Lou replied. "I
think Madeleine Zimmer is my new idol."

"She was perfectly cast," Connor agreed. "I *did*
feel like she was a little *handsy* with her acting,
though. I kind of wanted her to just stand still and
sing."

I nodded, although I hadn't really noticed. To
be honest, I had been so excited to be back in a
Broadway theater, I could hardly begin to think
about anyone's acting technique.

"But don't get me wrong," Connor continued, "she's an actual goddess."

I looked over to Lou, who smiled politely.

"So what else are you seeing?" he continued.

"We're going to see *Megaphone* tonight," I said.

"Aw, it's super fun." Imani smiled. "I'll be interested to see what you think about the choreography."

"Yeah," Connor murmured, rubbing the ends of his chopsticks together, causing tiny particles of wood dust to sprinkle onto his lap. "I have to say, I liked it more off-Broadway. I think it loses the *immersive, environmental* quality in that big house."

I nodded meaningfully, hoping it looked like I had any idea what he was talking about.

"Are you going to be able to see *Molly Coddle* at Threshold Arts?" Imani asked, looking over to Lou.

"No . . . I don't think so," she mumbled.

"Oh, you should try and see it if you have time," Imani pushed on. "It's playing in their black box space until the end of the month and is a must-see. Also, Forrest Donovan is in it. He is *beyond*."

"He's so cute," Connor added.

"Oh!" Lou laughed nervously.

While we talked about almost everything, Lou

and I were still not in the place where we were comfortable discussing our crushes.

"Well you have to see it," Imani continued. "That and *The Big Apple* were my favorite sho—" Her lips froze in an *o* as everyone's eyes darted across the table to me. Suddenly the restaurant seemed to fall dead silent. The tinkling of soup spoons and water glasses halted. You could practically hear a chopstick drop.

"Where's our food?" Connor finally blurted out, twisting his head to the sushi bar, trying to get the attention of the ancient man stacking pink hunks of fish.

"That and *The Big Apple* were what?" I asked tentatively.

"Um, nothing," Imani said, fiddling with the row of skinny bracelets on her wrist. "I mean, it was . . . cute."

"Yeah," Connor said, slowly turning back to us. "Really nice . . . sets, I guess. The way they do the subway effect is kind of . . . neat." They both shifted uncomfortably in their chairs. "To be honest, they could have done without an intermission," he began to ramble. "The second act was ten to fifteen minutes too long, if you ask me, and the—"

"Guys, it's okay," I said, cutting him off. "You're allowed to like *The Big Apple*. In fact," I said, straightening my back, "I'm totally over the whole thing. I hope *everyone* thinks it's amazing."

I tried to sound as confident as Imani and Connor. I don't think anyone believed me.

"Speaking of amazing," Imani said, hurrying to change the subject. "How was *Into The Woods*? Those pictures you texted us were adorable."

I looked over at Lou. With all this talk of edgy new theater, our little musical seemed rather small.

"It was great," she said tentatively.

I knew Lou was probably thinking the same thing as me.

"I'm so jealous," Imani said to Lou. "Little Red is my number one dream role."

"How was your Witch?" Connor snorted. "That's *my* number one dream role."

"Such a diva," I replied. "You'd love her."

"Well, you guys would have been really proud," Lou chimed in. "Jack was pretty incredible."

Connor and Imani both tilted their heads and made little "awww" sounds.

"And, Connor, you would have totally approved," Lou said smartly. "There was a real . . . *stillness* to his work. Definitely not *hands-y* at all."

Connor's eyes narrowed as I bit the inside of my cheek. He was unreadable for a moment, but then a smirk began to form on his face.

"Ohhh, *toss, toss,*" Connor said, flipping imaginary hair off his shoulders like Glinda in *Wicked*.

We all burst out laughing.

"I like this one," he said, pointing a chopstick at Lou. "You sure you don't want to stay in New York? I collect sassy friends."

After every sip of tea had been slurped and every grain of rice devoured, we bundled up and clenched our teeth, stepping back into the polar chill of midtown. We trudged down the block to Schmackary's Cookies, where that week Broadway actors had swapped roles with the waitstaff to raise money for charity. Today the cast of *Aladdin* was serving up sweet treats. We snapped a few pictures, dropped some dollars in their bucket, and scooted up to a table. The smell of sugar cookies and peanut butter brownies wafted through the air as we sat giggling, Lou and Connor trading wisecracks.

"I'd order the red velvet," Lou whined in a cockney accent (her best attempt at Mrs. Lovett from *Sweeney Todd*), "but I fear they might be . . . *crummy.*"

"Let's be honest," Connor said with a chuckle, dipping his Schmacker-doodle into a glass of milk, "*this* is the only time you'll catch me *dunking.*"

I laughed out loud, watching my two worlds collide in such a delicious way.

"So what's next for you?" Imani leaned in as Connor and Lou continued their pun game. "Any projects coming up in the new year?"

Projects, I thought, committing the word to memory. That did sound way more sophisticated than *shows*.

"Yeah, maybe," I said, blowing into my hot chocolate. "Our school is doing *Guys and Dolls*, but to be honest, it might be kind of stupid."

Hearing the words *Guys and Dolls*, Lou halted her conversation.

"Well, not stupid," I backtracked. "It's just our director, Mrs. Wagner, is kind of lame. Last semester she spent more time talking about her upcoming ski trip than she did rehearsing our holiday concert."

"I thought you loved *Guys and Dolls*," Lou said somewhat accusingly.

"No, I mean, it's a classic," I said, shrugging. "I just feel like every theater in America does that show. It's kind of old-timey, you know?" Connor and Imani nodded in agreement. "I just wish it was a little more . . . *trendy*."

"Maybe you could all play your own instruments," Connor said deadpan. "Or have the guys play the dolls and the dolls play the guys."

Imani rolled her eyes. "Let's talk about casting. Jack, who would you want to play? Nathan Detroit or Sky Masterson?"

"Are you kidding?" Connor snorted. "Could you imagine our little Jacky crooning and being all serious? He's obviously a Nathan."

While I happened to agree, was it that obvious that I wasn't "leading man" material?

"Well, what about you?" Imani said, looking over at Lou. "Who are you auditioning for? Adelaide or Sarah Brown?"

"Oh, definitely Adelaide," Lou said. "She's, like, in the top three best roles for girls in musical theater."

Lou was right. She'd be the perfect Adelaide.

Not only would she get a ton of laugh lines but she'd also get to belt the big Act 1 showstopper.

Back on the street we said our good-byes. Imani had a jazz-funk class to catch at Broadway Dance Center just up the block, and Connor had dinner at his stepdad's on the Upper East Side.

"It was so nice seeing you," we said through scarf-muffled hugs.

"Enjoy Shaker Heights!" Imani exclaimed.

"Right," I groaned. "We'll try."

"I'm serious," Imani said, giving my shoulder a little punch. "Not gonna lie, I'm a little bit jealous. I miss my old house in Michigan."

"Yeah, you guys are so lucky," Connor huffed, "I bet it looks *gorge* in Ohio around the holidays. When it snows here, it goes from *White Christmas* to *Les Miz* in like five minutes."

Lou and I waved good-bye, smiling as we watched our friends walk down the salt-sprinkled pavement. I inhaled deeply, taking in the cold December air and smells of cinnamon sugar nut cart vendors. As we began our walk to the C train, a sense of relief washed over me. My friend mixer had been a success. Looking around the bustling streets, a warm feeling began to grow in my chest. While the noisy and crowded sidewalks were something real New Yorkers always complained about, where else in the world could you see anything like it? Watching Lou gawk at every horse-drawn carriage and street cartoonist reminded me how lucky I was to grow up in a place like this. *One day we'll live here for good*, I thought, *even if it feels like a million calendars away.*

As the light changed I opened my mouth to speak but was stopped dead in my tracks. Walking up the subway stairs across the street, chatting with his mom, was the last person on earth I wanted to see: the person who made that warm feeling in my chest turn cold; the person who made me unable to feel anything but overwhelming jealousy. It was Corey Taylor, the kid who replaced me in *The Big Apple*.

Three

-LOUISA-

I was replaying our afternoon with Jack's friends in my head as we approached the corner of 44th Street and Eighth Avenue—Connor's sassy humor, Imani's smarts and style, and the way I went from feeling totally intimidated by them at first to feeling like we'd been lifelong friends by the time we got to Schmackary's—when Jack suddenly stopped short, causing a young woman to bump into us.

"Ugh, *excuse* me," she muttered, shimmying past us in her black yoga pants and puffy coat.

Jack was so fixated on something across the street that I stopped thinking about his super-cool

theater friends and grabbed his elbow to steer
him toward the curb, away from the middle of the
sidewalk.

"Jack," I said, "what are you looking at?"

I followed his gaze across 44th Street toward
the subway entrance. A young boy and a woman
who looked like his mother were waiting for
the light to change, meaning that in just a few
moments they would be on our side of the street.

Jack spoke out of the corner of his mouth,
keeping his eyes on the mother-son pair.

"That's Corey Taylor," he said quietly, his jaw
tensing. "That's the kid who took over my part in
The Big Apple."

My reaction must have been a little too obvious
because Jack pinched my hand and hissed, "Play it
cool, Lou. They see us."

And sure enough, here they came, both smiling
a little too brightly on this overcast December day.
I did my best to wear my meeting-new-people face,
instead of my you-stole-something-precious-from-
my-best-friend face.

"Well, hello there, *Jack*!" exclaimed Corey's
mom. "What a *surprise*! We didn't know you were in
town!"

Why would you? I thought, looking at the two of them and wondering just how uncomfortable Jack was feeling. *You think you're the first people Jack's going to call when he plans a visit?*

"Well, it was really last-minute," Jack fibbed, smiling politely. "My parents' friends suggested we come for New Year's and stay in their apartment since they're in Puerto Rico."

"Cool!" chirped Corey, nodding vigorously. While I remembered Jack telling me at one point that the kid who replaced him was ten years old, in person he looked even younger—like eight. He had that scrubbed look of a kid in a Toaster Strudel commercial—big, round eyes, perfect haircut, rosy cheeks. The way he said "Cool!" made me think he'd said it on camera (perhaps in a Toaster Strudel commercial).

My inspection of Corey was interrupted by his mom's hand jutting toward me.

"*Hi*, I'm Carol *Taylor*, and this is my son *Corey*."

She had this bizarre way of emphasizing certain words.

"Hi," I said, shaking Carol's hand and nodding toward Corey, who gave me a little wave, "I'm Louisa, but everybody calls me Lou." For some reason I was okay telling her my nickname. Maybe because she didn't intimidate me at all; I think she annoyed me.

"*So* nice to meet you," said Carol. "Are you visiting as *well*?"

"Yeah, I live in Shaker Heights, too," I said. "Jack and I go to the same school."

I looked over at Jack, who was now biting the inside of his lip.

"Cool!" Corey chirped again.

"How nice that you *both* get to be in *New York* at this time of year," said Carol. She placed a hand on top of Corey's head.

"We haven't had much of a chance to celebrate the holidays, what with this guy's *show* schedule." She tousled his hair, but then immediately smoothed it back into place.

"Yeah, I'm sure," mumbled Jack, nodding but not really making eye contact with anyone.

"Of course," Carol answered emphatically, "you know all about Broadway holiday schedules, you old *pro*, you."

Jack replied with a tight-lipped smile.

"Will you guys have tomorrow off, at least?" I asked, sensing that Jack wasn't going to bring much to the conversation.

"No!" Corey howled, rolling his eyes cartoonishly. "Can you believe it? New Year's Eve and we have to *work*!"

"But of course we're *grateful*, aren't we, Corey?" Carol added quickly. "We don't *ever* want to take the job for *granted*."

"Right!" Corey bleated. "Totally!"

Jack started to shift his feet, making me think he was about to get us out of this awkward situation, when Carol suddenly inhaled sharply.

"*Wait a second!*" She held up her hands dramatically, like she was putting on the brakes to an exciting conversation that no one was actually having.

"We have *two* tickets to tomorrow's matinee that we were going to give to Corey's cousins, but they *both* came down with strep two days ago and are *highly* contagious."

"Yeah, so gross!" Corey yipped in confirmation.

"Would you and Louisa like to use the tickets *instead*?"

I knew I was in no position to answer that question, so I looked over at Jack, who pursed his lips and opened his eyes wide. After a short pause, he spoke.

"That ... would be amazing," he replied so convincingly that I started to think I'd misread his body language up to that point. He looked over at me expectantly.

"Whaddya say, Lou? You wanna go?"

I looked back at Carol and Corey, who wore the expressions of game-show contestants waiting to find out if they've given the correct answer.

"I ... would love to!" I said enthusiastically. "Thanks so much!"

Carol and Corey demonstrated their excitement with simultaneous bouncing.

"How *wonderful!*" Carol gushed.

"Yeah," said Jack, "thanks, Mrs. Taylor."

"Call me Carol, *please!*"

"Thanks ... Carol."

Corey suddenly stretched out his arms and moved toward Jack. The next thing I knew he was hugging him tightly.

"I'm so glad you're coming!"

Carol placed a hand on her chest, clearly moved by her perfect son's gesture of affection.

"You have *no* idea, Jack," Carol said, beaming,

"how much Corey looks up to you. You're pretty much *the* reason we got into this business in the first place."

I looked at Corey, who, though still smiling, now looked a little embarrassed. Jack gave a nervous laugh.

"Wow," was all he could muster.

"Yep," Carol continued, "it was seeing you in *Mary Poppins* that did it for him. 'Member, Cor?" She lifted up her son's chin to face her.

"You turned to me at intermission and said, 'Mom, I want to be like *that* boy up there.'"

"Yeah, I did," Corey said, softly. His voice had dipped below screech level for the first time in the conversation. It was actually kind of sweet. He and his mom had come on so strong at first, but now I realized it was because they were genuinely excited to see Jack and wanted to impress him. They were suddenly less annoying.

"You *know*," Carol said, looking at me, "everyone was *so* disappointed when Jack couldn't come out a couple months ago to be the vacation swing. Especially since he'd helped create the show from the beginning—"

"Yeah, that was too bad," Jack interrupted, a

sudden urgency in his voice, "but at least now I'll finally get to see the show!"

"That's *right!*" Carol said, grabbing Corey's hand and flashing us one last smile.

"All right, well—see you *tomorrow!* Happy New Year, *almost!*"

Jack and I grinned and waved good-bye as the two of them disappeared into the throng of pedestrians maneuvering up and down Eighth Avenue.

Once they were out of sight, I turned to Jack, desperate to get his take on the last two minutes.

"That was kind of crazy, huh?" I asked, nudging his shoulder. "I mean, I wasn't sure if you were going to say yes to those tickets. But you clearly made their day when you did." Jack gave a halfhearted laugh.

"Yeah, I guess," Jack said, crouching down to retie his bootlaces.

"You know, even though they're a little intense, Carol and Corey obviously think you're, like, the best thing ever. It's kinda cute how much of a star you are to them."

"It's adorable," Jack replied sarcastically as he stood back up. "Let's get going; it's cold." He leaned into the wind and marched quickly toward the corner.

"Whoa, slow down!" I called out, skip-walking to keep up with him as he dodged pedestrians like a character in a video game.

"Sorry," he called back over his shoulder as he crossed 44th Street, "it's just we should probably hurry if we want to eat dinner before we see *Megaphone.*"

Didn't we just have lunch? I thought, searching my pockets for my MetroCard as Jack disappeared down the stairs leading to the subway. It seemed like catching the train was suddenly the most important thing he'd ever done. It also seemed like he was trying to get away from me—which was weird, since we were basically stuck with each other.

"Hey—are you okay?" I asked, catching up with him at the bottom of the stairs.

"Totally," said Jack, now rushing toward the turnstiles.

We swiped our MetroCards and raced toward the signs for the uptown C train.

"Are you sure?" I gasped, out of breath from practically chasing my friend down to the subway platform. "You don't *seem* okay—"

Jack turned abruptly to face me, wearing an expression I couldn't quite read. He was smiling, sort of, but his eyes were not.

"Hey, can we not talk for a while?"

Jack had never asked me to stop talking, and I was instantly embarrassed.

"Oh. Sure."

I must have looked a little stung, because Jack's face softened.

"Sorry, it's just . . . I'm really tired. I kinda want to be quiet for a bit, if that's all right."

"Yeah. Totally."

We waited for the train for five minutes, then rode all the way to 81st Street in complete silence, tense and uneasy. I figured I'd done something wrong. But what?

"Hey there!" Mrs. Goodrich greeted us as we arrived back at the apartment. "Your father is getting stuff for dinner at Fairway," she said, helping us hang up our bags, hats, and scarves. "I had a craving for their pumpkin ravioli. It cooks up really fast, so we'll be able to eat and get to *Megaphone* in plenty of time."

I looked to Jack, hoping this culinary news would brighten his mood, but he was concentrating intensely on untying his boots. Mrs. Goodrich didn't notice that her son was out of sorts as she continued, "So . . . I hear you two are seeing *The Big Apple* tomorrow?"

Not surprisingly, an already tense Jack grew tenser.

News travels fast in this city, I thought.

"How did you hear—" he began, kicking off a remaining boot.

"I just got a call from Carol Taylor," Mrs. Goodrich explained. "She said she ran into you guys and offered you tickets to tomorrow's matinee, but that she forgot to tell you they'll be held at the box office under Corey's name. Boy, do they love you! She said you were Corey's *idol*."

She was regarding Jack with a mix of curiosity and surprise. Attending a matinee performance of *The Big Apple* was certainly not an event she'd been expecting in our itinerary, either. Jack started to bite the inside of his lip again.

"Jack," I began carefully, "are you . . . are you *sure* you're okay about seeing the show tomorrow?"

He looked at me, took a deep breath, and

said, "I've decided I'm not going to see the show tomorrow."

I blinked rapidly. Mrs. Goodrich looked uneasy.

"You're not?" she asked tentatively.

"No."

"But . . . you told them you'd take the tickets."

"You and Lou can go together," Jack suggested, his tone measured and deliberate. "I don't need to see *The Big Apple*. I mean, if I were a vacation swing, that would be different, but I don't want to just sit there as an audience member and have that be the only reason I'm there."

"I'm sorry, Jack, but if you accepted Mrs. Taylor's offer, you have to—"

"*I'm not going*," Jack repeated forcefully.

Mrs. Goodrich kept her gaze fixed on Jack, and the air in the room changed in the way air changes when a fight is about to start. I knew it was time for me to disappear.

"I'm going to go call my parents," I announced. "I haven't talked to them since we got here."

"Alright, Lou," Mrs. Goodrich said quietly. "Why don't you use the guest bedroom? You can watch the TV in there, too, if you want."

I grabbed my backpack from one of the hooks

by the door and glanced furtively at Jack, who was now staring angrily at his hands.

"Okay," I said, and hurried down the hallway. There were too many thoughts in my head, and I didn't trust any of them. On the one hand, Mrs. Goodrich was right—it didn't seem polite to accept an offer from the Taylors and then not follow through, no matter how overbearing they were. But on the other hand, I had never been in Jack's position before; I'd never had something so important—possibly life-changing—taken away from me, so how could I know what that felt like? Even though he'd assured Connor and Imani that he was "totally over the whole thing," it was now very clear that he was not, and it seemed unfair of me to judge his decision not to see the show. Especially since sometimes, being mad or jealous about something just felt right. And felt deserved. But here was the most confusing part: As bad as I felt for Jack at this moment, the truth was that if he hadn't been fired from *The Big Apple* in the first place, he never would have moved to Shaker Heights. And I never would have met him. The thing that caused him all that pain basically delivered him to my doorstep.

How could I make sense of that?

As Jack's and Mrs. Goodrich's voices began to
rise in their heated exchange down the hall, a wave
of exhaustion washed over me. Our afternoon had
taken its toll. I reached into my backpack for my
cell phone and dialed "Home," anticipating the
relief I'd feel once I'd shared all the events of my
trip. After three rings, my mom answered.

"Oh my goodness, we're just about to play Taboo
with Uncle Dan and Tina, but tell me quick—are
you having a great time?" she asked, and the pure
excitement in her voice, plus the sound of someone
in the background testing out the Taboo buzzer,
made me rethink what I'd planned to say. There
would be time enough to tell her everything.

"Yes," I replied, turning on the television and
lying down on the guest bed, "it's been quite an
adventure."

-JACK-

"Then why did you tell them you wanted to go?" my mom said, crossing her arms. "You could have easily told them you already had plans."

I couldn't believe my ears. My own mother was actually encouraging me to lie!

"They trapped me!" I shouted. "I wanted to get out of there, and I didn't know what else to say."

"They weren't trying to trap you," my mom said with a frown. "They were trying to include you. Carol was just saying how much Corey looks up to you. He's seen your shows and was probably excited to get to perform for you."

"That's even worse!" I clenched my jaw, digging

my heels angrily into the carpet. "How is that supposed to make me feel better?"

"He just wants you to like him the way he likes you."

"Why do I have to like him?!" I blurted out. "If there's one person in this entire world that I'm allowed to dislike, no questions asked, I think it should be him!"

"Jack! That's an unkind thing to say!" she said. "Maybe seeing the show will be good for you. Maybe you'll get some closure and find a lesson in all of this."

"What lesson?!" I screamed, making her eyebrows rise. "That life sucks, and some younger, cuter, bratty kid is probably going to take your job?"

"Jack!" She hushed me fiercely, gesturing toward the room where Lou was sitting nervously, no doubt.

"I just . . ." I felt my throat tighten. All the thoughts and anger and worries of the day seemed to be piling up like Jenga pieces. I knew all it would take was a nudge in the wrong direction, and I'd be done. "I just don't want to pretend to be happy in front of all those people."

As the words left my mouth I knew I'd lost my grip. I turned away from her and dove onto the couch, smushing my face into the armrest. My mom let out a sigh. I listened as her socks slowly brushed across the carpet. I felt the sinking of the couch cushion as she nestled up next to me.

"Ah, Jack." She exhaled, beginning to scratch my back. "I don't know what to tell you. Part of me thinks you should honor your commitment, but I also don't want you to torture yourself."

We sat in silence for a while, the seconds counted by soft scratches of fingernails against my cotton T-shirt. I pressed my forehead into the brown upholstery, replaying the meeting with Corey and his mom. *If only we'd talked to Connor and Imani longer*, I kept thinking. *If only we'd taken a different subway line home.*

"I worry sometimes, Jack. I worry that your dad and I might have made a mistake, letting you work in this adult world while you were still a kid," my mom said softly. "It's one of the reasons we moved to Shaker Heights. Losing a job and the feelings that come with that—that's a lot for a twelve-year-old to deal with."

Listening to her somehow made me even

sadder. Of course I hated getting fired, but what would my life have been like if I hadn't had the chance to work on Broadway?

"If you don't want to see *The Big Apple*, I'll support you, of course," my mom said finally. "But I can't help thinking it might be good for you to see it. To be reminded that it's just a show and not this big scary thing that's always following you."

She smoothed my hair and stood up from the couch.

"Either way, we should let them know before we leave tonight."

"You do know I would have supported you no matter what," Lou declared the next day, practically doing bell kicks as we crossed Times Square. "But now that we're here, I'm really glad you decided to see the show."

The Palace Theatre was located in the heart of the theater district. Over the years its tenants ranged from *Oklahoma!* to *Beauty and the Beast* to *Legally Blonde*, making it one of the most iconic Broadway houses, always depicted in postcard photos and snow globes.

"We'll see." I shrugged, stepping up onto the curb. "If nothing else, I *do* want to see how they do the subway effect at the end of Act One."

"You gonna be okay, Jack Sprat?" my dad asked, handing us our tickets.

I looked up at the giant signs framing the entrance, quotes from the theater critics proclaiming *"Heart-Racing!" "Eye-Popping!"* and *"Delicious!"* The walls were plastered with production photos, shots of *Corey* crouched on a curb, *Corey* under the Brooklyn Bridge with the actress who played his mom, *Corey* jumping over a subway turnstile. His eyes seemed to be staring directly at me, teasing, as if to say, "Pretty cool, right? Remember when this was *almost* you?"

"I think I'll be okay," I said in a shaky voice.

"I told him if it gets too intense, we can totally leave at intermission," Lou assured my dad. "I'm more than happy to hear the second act when the cast recording comes out next month."

We'd come this far; I knew I might as well face the music. And no matter what she claimed, Lou would be disappointed if I dragged her out halfway through.

"Well, enjoy the show," my mom said, kissing

the top of my head. "Text us when you get out."

As we entered the theater we were greeted
by friendly ushers gently herding us past
merchandise stands hawking *Big Apple* T-shirts,
mugs, and sippy cups. We made our way down the
red-and-gold carpet to a pair of seats in row G. On
our previous two trips to Broadway shows, Lou and
I had made a game of going through the Playbill
and pointing out every cast member that I knew.
It was an activity that always ended in laughter
because, more often than not, I didn't really *know*
them.

Well, I once stood behind her at Schnippers, I'd say,
or *I saw him totally bite it on the stairs at the 42nd
Street subway station.*

"Wanna tell me about who came late
to rehearsal or had bad breath?" Lou asked
encouragingly, clutching her Playbill like a golden
ticket.

"Is it okay if I pass?" I said, forcing a smile.

"Of course," Lou replied. "I'll just assume that
because they're on Broadway, everyone has a good
work ethic and perfect dental hygiene."

The Big Apple didn't begin with an overture like most musicals typically do, rather the single voice of a child.

"One song, one song worth singing..."

I shivered in my seat. A pin spot beamed down on Corey dressed as the character of Hudson, looking even tinier and more adorable than he did in person. As he sang, the lighting began to shift. Projections of a passing subway *whoosh*ed past him. Suddenly the orchestra kicked in, and we were transported from the graffiti-scrawled subway tunnels to a bustling Times Square complete with actors riding Citi Bikes, dancers dressed as furry mascots, and even a life-size "Big Apple" double-decker bus.

Although the production looked just as epic as the critics had described, the only thing I could concentrate on was Corey. I watched as he maneuvered his way through staging I remembered learning in those early rehearsals. It all came rushing back to me—dashing stage right to fake-collide with a woman carrying shopping bags, hopping stage left over an imaginary puddle, stealing a hot dog off a street cart upstage. I wondered if Lou was paying as much attention to

Corey and his blocking as I was. I'm sure everyone in the audience was only thinking what a great job he was doing.

As the first act whizzed by, I kept forcing myself to concentrate and enjoy the show, but it got harder and harder to do. I hadn't realized how many lines I'd memorized until a new one would spring up and startle me. Finally, when a giant set piece that was supposed to be the inside of a subway car tracked onstage, I knew we were close to intermission. The final scene involved Hudson being chased through a train by a pair of police officers. A strip of stage became a treadmill with Corey and the officers running one way while passengers and metal train car doors zipped by in the other direction. As the intermission house lights sprung to life, the audience roared with applause. It pained me to admit, it was one of the best-choreographed sequences I'd ever seen on a Broadway stage.

"How ya doin', friend?" Lou asked as an elderly couple squeezed past us.

"I'm fine," I said, ducking my head to avoid being swatted by their rolled-up programs. "It's cool, right?"

"Definitely," Lou confided. "Although Connor *did*

say the second act kind of drags, so we'll just have to see."

Connor was wrong; the second act was even better than the first. I caught Lou stifling laughter, still trying to play the role of the biased, supportive friend. In the final scene where Hudson's mother runs onstage and hugs him, a tiny whimper escaped from her lips. She covered it immediately by pretending to clear her throat. The curtain fell, and the audience leaped to its feet, an immediate standing ovation. Lou hesitated, but followed my lead as I stood and cheered for the ensemble, strutting from the wings to take their bows.

"That was really good," I mumbled as we made our way up the aisle, crammed with school groups and patrons clutching soggy Kleenexes.

"It was," Lou agreed. "Thanks for taking me."

"Of course," I said, so many thoughts racing through my head.

We hung a right at the corner, nearing the stage door. A cluster of people had already formed a line against the steel barricades, clutching their glossy Playbills and cell phones. Some were even armed with Sharpies, already uncapped and waiting for the cast to emerge. Lou stopped suddenly, grabbing my hand.

"Jack," she said. "Are you sure you don't want to just go home? We can say we had to meet your parents for a dinner reservation or something."

"No," I said, speaking over the blaring of car horns and audience chatter. "We should at least say thanks to Corey for getting us the tickets."

Lou looked at me intently, searching for a signal or something to let her know that I was going to be okay.

"Thanks for being sensitive, though." I half laughed. "But I'm good now. You don't have to worry about me."

"Okay," she said, nodding. "Anytime."

We gave our name to the security guard and were ushered down a narrow staircase, my heart beating faster with every step.

"Well, look who it is!" a voice called from behind us. We turned to find Kip, the *Big Apple* stage manager whose mouth hung open in disbelief. "You've gotten so big! You're like a little man now!"

"Haha, it's true!" I said, hugging him, deciding not to mention that compared to the rest of the kids in my class, I was still pretty short.

A parade of *hellos* and *congratulations* soon followed. Everyone who rounded the corner said essentially the same thing: "Look at how grown-up you are!" or "In a couple years you should come back and play the Taxi Driver!"

"I'm so proud of you guys," I kept repeating. "You were incredible!"

The more hands I shook and the more waists I hugged, the more I began to notice what was going on. Panic seemed to flash across my old castmates' faces as they saw me standing in the greenroom—*oh jeez, I hope this kid is all right.* I tried my best to make the situation less awkward, tried to make everyone more comfortable by bombarding them with compliments, asking them about their spouses, their kids, their pets. I knew it would make everyone feel better if I seemed okay.

But all this well-wishing was just a dress rehearsal. I knew the big show would be when Corey skipped around the corner and I'd have to congratulate him. I'd practiced with Lou exactly what I was going to say. "Congrats, buddy. You were so great!" I repeated it like lines for an audition. "Congrats, buddy. You were *SO* great."

I was snapping a picture of Lou and Ryan
Turner, a dancer from the show who was Lou's
favorite, when I felt a pair of arms wrap around my
neck. I turned to see that I was being hugged by
Corey.

"Hey there, buddy, you were . . . you were . . ."
I stammered, taken off guard. *You were so great,*
a tiny voice rang in my head. *You were so great.*
You were so great. But the words felt lodged in my
throat like a popcorn kernel.

"You were so great!" Lou chimed in, saving the
day.

"Thanks!" Corey cooed, his red-cheeked face
beaming up at us. "Didja like it?" he squawked.

"Y-yup." I gulped. "I did."

"Cool!" he cheered, his smile spreading wider
and wider. "I just got an Xbox in my dressing
room," he said, abruptly changing the subject.
"Have you played *Plants vs. Zombies*?"

"Um, I . . . haven't," I croaked.

"It's so cool!"

I felt Lou's boot pressing up against mine.

"You remember my friend Lou, right?" I asked.

"Yeah!" He grinned.

"Good to see you again," Lou said eloquently.

"I was so impressed with your performance. You are quite the little singer."

Lou had apparently been practicing, too. She looked over at me, raising her eyebrows slightly as if to cue me in on a dropped line.

"Sh-sh-yeah," I said, completely tongue-tied.

"Thanks!" he chirped.

We pushed our way out of the stage door and right into the crowds who had started gathering for the big New Year's Eve ball drop in Times Square. Police officers were setting up metal barricades, and tourists were huddled together, pointing at billboards and laughing, ready to brave the cold for the next seven hours. Men wearing wacky glittered hats pushed shopping carts stuffed with merchandise: neon glasses, plastic horns, and other souvenirs that would be worthless the next morning. We passed the big stage on 43rd, where crew guys were setting up speakers and lights, prepping for the evening's performances. Lou's face lit up, but catching my glance, she quickly snapped back to her serious New Yorker face.

"I know, I know," she grumbled. "Avoiding Times Square on New Year's is probably lesson number *one*, right?"

I was so proud.

That night we were joined by a few of my parents' friends, toasting the New Year from the quiet of the Upper West Side. My mom had spent the evening preparing and photographing vegan appetizers for her food blog. We stuffed our faces with eggplant-lentil fritters and cashew-cauliflower crostini as the New Year's broadcast blared in the background. We played board games and chugged sparkling apple cider, making bets about who could stay up the latest.

"I'll make it till the ball drops."

"That's nothing. I bet I can stay up until two in the morning."

"Until we have to go to the airport!"

Truthfully, neither of us lasted very long, not even close to midnight. I don't think we realized how exhausting this vacation had been until the next day at the airport when my dad suggested we scroll through the camera roll on my mom's phone. Sure enough, there it was, a series of photos, the two of us slumped on the couch,

Lou's sleeping head resting on my shoulder, our noisemakers and blow horns scattered by our sides. "I couldn't resist!" my mom confessed.

Lou and I shared a row for the flight back to Cleveland, our elbows fighting for armrest real estate.

"For the first time I think I understand the expression 'I need a vacation from my vacation,'" I said in a sleepy voice.

"I get what you mean," Lou replied. "I can't believe how much we crammed into just a few days."

"What was your favorite thing we did?" I asked.

"Oh, definitely getting to go backstage at *Let's Make a Toast!*" Lou said quickly. "Or maybe getting to meet your friends," she wavered. "Orrrr . . ."

"The Schmackary's cookies," we said in unison.

For a while we sat in silence, the engine humming as we sliced through the clouds.

"Thanks for being my wingman at *The Big Apple* yesterday," I said finally.

"Of course. I'm glad you brought me." She smiled. "So was your mom right? Do you feel any better after seeing it? Did you get some closure?"

Honestly, I thought, *I'm not sure.* It was hard to watch, and what made it worse was realizing how perfectly it chugged along without me.

"Sure." I shrugged. "I feel like Corey was really different from me, a lot younger, and that was good to be reminded of," I said, echoing something I'd heard her say earlier.

"Totally." She nodded. "Although I do have to admit, it made me really wish I could have seen you in it."

I smiled, looking down at my tray table.

"Like, Corey was adorable and everything, but I would have liked to see you bring some of that token Jack Goodrich snark to the role," she said, elbowing me. "I bet you were amazing."

"Thanks," I said.

"And for what it's worth," she continued, "I think facing all those people and saying all those nice things kind of gave you your power back."

I looked up. "What do you mean?"

"I don't know," she said with a shrug. "I just mean, you acted like a grown-up. Like you weren't afraid to face what happened to you."

"Yeah." I sighed. "Well, not to Corey. I didn't

even say congratulations. He must think I'm such a jerk."

"He's a kid," Lou said. "I'm sure he didn't even notice. I'm sure you'll find a way to tell him eventually."

"Yeah." I squinted, looking away from her. I thought about Corey and my friends back in New York, about theaters and sidewalks dusted with confetti. Suddenly a thought emerged in my head. I wasn't sure if it counted as a lesson, but it certainly felt important. If I hadn't been fired from *The Big Apple*, I wouldn't have had Lou to see it with. I turned back but found her preoccupied, her face pressed against the window, bidding a final farewell to the parks and buildings that she dreamed of knowing. *One day, we'll be back*, I thought. But for now it was time to begin a new year in Shaker Heights.

-LOUISA-

The buzzer on my alarm clock felt like a cruel joke. Even though Jack and I had returned from our trip two days ago, I was still exhausted. The thought of getting up and going back to school was, well . . . awful. What could possibly happen today that would remotely compare to the adventures we'd had in New York? Unless Idina Menzel was planning on surprising us in our homeroom with a private concert of songs from *Frozen*, there was literally nothing to look forward to until bedtime, and I was pretty sure Idina was too busy being a star to make any detours to Shaker Heights Middle School. I heard my mom making my lunch downstairs, and I thought about the pork soup dumplings I'd had just days earlier at Shanghai Café Deluxe, the Goodriches' favorite restaurant in Chinatown. Compared to those salty, soupy bites of pure magic, my usual turkey and lettuce on whole wheat was going to taste pretty boring today.

"Don't look so excited," my mom said sarcastically as I shuffled into the kitchen, squinting against the bright lights. She had the news going on the radio and was pouring what I guessed was probably her second cup of coffee. Mom considered herself a morning person, which I considered an alien species all its own.

"I don't want to go back to school," I said huskily. My body was awake, but my voice was not.

"Just think how much fun it will be to tell all your friends about your trip!" she said cheerfully, pouring me a glass of orange juice.

"They won't care about the things I care about," I said. "They'll just want to know if I went to a Yankees game. Or if I got mugged."

"The Yankees aren't playing this time of year."

Dad brushed past me on his way to the coffeepot, saying, "But you might get asked if you saw the Giants play. And thanks for reminding me: *Did* you get mugged?"

Mom laughed. I rolled my eyes.

At 7:15 a.m. I arrived at the bus stop to find Jack already there, shivering in the morning darkness.

"Was New York a dream?" I joked through chattering teeth. "Did our trip even happen?"

"Oh, it happened," said Jack, burying his face in his scarf. "Corey Taylor keeps sending me texts about what Xbox games I should buy."

"Aww," I teased, "he wants to be your friend."

"Lucky me."

The bus pulled up to the curb, and Jack and I exchanged mournful looks.

"Let's do this." I sighed.

As we boarded, a familiar voice called to us from the back, "Lou! Jack! Come here!"

Jenny Westcott, outfitted in a new coat, hat, scarf, and gloves, looked like she'd stepped out of a department store window. Her holiday wish list had been made up entirely of clothing and accessories, and it looked like this Christmas had been particularly good to her. She got up from her seat and gave us each a hug. The day suddenly got a little brighter as I realized I did have something (or rather, someone) to look forward to: Jenny.

"So listen, Jack," she said, making room for me next to her on the seat, "Lou told me all about your big city trip on the phone last night, but what I'm *most* interested in is the *present* you guys apparently got me?" Jenny flashed her signature playful grin, making Jack laugh.

"Of course, how could I forget?" Jack replied, sitting across the aisle and digging in his bag.

"I hope you like it," I said, grabbing Jenny's hand excitedly as Jack produced a plastic shopping bag bearing the "I Love NY" logo. He handed it to Jenny, who squeezed it, trying to guess its contents.

"Well, I can tell it's clothing," she said, "so I already like it."

She reached into the bag and pulled out a folded pink V-neck T-shirt with a logo that made her shriek.

"The American Ballet Theatre! You *guys!*"

American Ballet Theatre (or ABT) was to Jenny what Broadway was to us—it was the dance company that represented everything she trained for, dreamed about, aspired to achieve. Jack and I didn't go to the ballet when we were in New York, but we still took a special trip to Lincoln Center so that we could get her the T-shirt from the gift shop.

"I'll wear it tomorrow," she said, blowing air-kisses at us and sliding the T-shirt back into the "I Love NY" bag. "I'd wear it today, but it will go better with different pants."

As I had predicted, Jack and I were greeted by our homeroom classmates with questions about our trip that really had nothing to do with our trip.

"Did you go to the top of the Empire State Building?"

"Did you meet Donald Trump?"

"Did you eat a lot of pizza?"

"Bagels?"

"Soft pretzels?"

"Did you get mugged?"

Leave it to Tanner Falzone to ask us about getting mugged. He looked a little disappointed when we said no.

I'll admit it did feel nice to receive that kind of attention from our classmates (minus Tanner's ridiculous question), even if they didn't know to ask me whether I'd sat in a Broadway star's dressing room and learned the secrets of her quick costume changes.

The Jack and Louisa Q&A came to an abrupt end, however, when Hilary Heaslip burst into the room, her eyes wide.

"You guys," she said urgently, making all of us turn our heads in her direction, "did you hear about Mrs. Wagner?"

I looked around at the faces of my classmates. Judging by their blank expressions, they had not.

"She had, like, a *major* skiing accident in Colorado," Hilary announced, making us all gasp.

"She's okay," she rushed to clarify. "I mean, I heard Mr. Gordon and Mrs. Silver talking in the hall, and they said she's gonna be okay eventually. But she broke, like, *everything*."

More gasps. Hilary fluttered her hands and shook her head.

"Okay, maybe not *everything*, but, like, a *lot* of bones. They say she's gonna be out for the rest of the *year*."

The classroom sprang to life with conversation as everyone began to speculate what was going to happen to Mrs. Wagner and what that meant for music class. Hilary seemed to be enjoying her role as messenger. It was like she was holding a press conference, with everyone directing their questions and comments at her.

"So who's going to teach music now?"

"Maybe we won't have to take it—maybe we'll get a free period?"

"My dad broke his leg skiing. Compound fracture."

"What's that?"

"When the bone sticks through the skin."

"Gross!"

"That's probably what happened to Mrs. Wagner."

"I like skiing in Vermont better."

Jenny turned around in her seat in front of me, her eyebrows raised in surprise.

"*Ouch*," she said, biting her bottom lip.

I looked across the room at Jack, who sat at his desk, grimacing. He caught me looking at him and mouthed the words *Oh no*.

I just shook my head in response.

He must have felt as guilty as I did, since it was only last week that we'd been complaining to Jack's New York friends about how we thought Mrs.

Wagner was "lame." I felt even more guilty as I wondered, with real concern, what her accident meant for our production of *Guys and Dolls*.

As Hilary continued holding court, our homeroom teacher, Mrs. Lamon, strode through the door, looking tired.

"I can see you've already heard about Mrs. Wagner," she said, setting down her bag and coffee mug. "Hilary, please take your seat, the school day has begun."

Hilary took her seat. Her time in the spotlight had ended.

"Here's what I can tell you: Mrs. Wagner suffered serious injuries while attempting to ski for the first time in Vail, Colorado," Mrs. Lamon explained. Then she sighed as she looked down at her desk. "I told her to stay on the bunny hill . . ." She snapped her head back up and continued: "But she is expected to make a full recovery, which is very good news. Even so, she will not be back for the rest of the year due to the extensive nature of her rehabilitation. So. I think it would be nice if we put together a get-well card from our class. Hilary, since you seem to have a vested interest in Mrs. Wagner's situation, will you please be in charge of putting that together?"

"Yes, Mrs. Lamon." Hilary beamed. She had become important, once again.

"As far as music class is concerned," Mrs. Lamon continued, "Mr. Hennessy has agreed to take over for the rest of the semester." I looked across the room at Jack again, and we exchanged more worried glances. Mr. Hennessy was our very sweet, very old accompanist, who rarely said more than "Which measure?" or "All righty" in response to Mrs. Wagner. It was hard to imagine him leading a class. It was even harder to imagine him directing a musical. And that's what made me raise my hand.

"Yes, Lou?"

"Is Mr. Hennessy going to be directing *Guys and Dolls*?"

"Actually, *no*," she replied, "a Shaker Heights alumna has been hired as Mrs. Wagner's replacement for the spring musical." She paused, and it looked like she might be trying to suppress a smile.

"I'm excited to see her again," she added coyly. "She hasn't been back here in a really long time."

Jack and I shared glance number three.

I was about to ask the next obvious question,

but Jenny beat me to the punch. Mrs. Lamon's vague response had clearly piqued more than just my own curiosity.

"Who is it?"

Mrs. Lamon cleared her throat and began shuffling papers on her desk.

"Her name is Belinda Grier," she said, using her usual teacher voice, "and you will all meet her in music class today. Now, would someone please help me pass out this paperwork? There's a lot of second semester business to cover."

The news of Mrs. Wagner and her mystery replacement (*not* Mr. Hennessy) overshadowed the rest of my morning, and I sat fidgeting through math and geography. But my agitation was nothing compared to Jenny's. During the four-minute break between geography and music, she ran up to me and Jack in the hallway, practically bursting with news.

"You guys are not going to believe this," she said, gripping her cell phone and waving it in our faces. *"My mom went to school with Belinda Grier."*

"Seriously?" said Jack.

"How did you figure that out?" I asked.

"As soon as Mrs. Lamon said her name, I was like, '*That sounds so familiar.*' And so in French class I was about to look her up on Google, but *then* I remembered it was my *mom* who's talked about her, so I texted her. Check it out."

Jenny tapped on her phone, then turned it around for us to read her text exchange as we walked to class.

JENNY: U KNOW A LADY NAMED BELINDA, RIGHT?

MOM: BELINDA GRIER?

JENNY: YA

MOM: I WENT TO SCHOOL WITH HER. SHE WAS THE STAR OF ALL OUR MUSICALS.

JENNY: SHE'S DIRECTING OUR MUSICAL!

MOM: WHAT HAPPENED TO MRS. WAGNER?

JENNY: SKI ACCIDENT. SHE'S OK, JUST OUT 4 SEMESTER.

MOM: OH DEAR.

JENNY: YOU LIKED BELINDA?

MOM: SHE WAS AMAZING. SHE HASN'T BEEN BACK HERE IN A REALLY LONG TIME.

JENNY: THAT'S WHAT MRS. LAMON SAID.

MOM: DOES MRS. LAMON KNOW YOU'RE TEXTING IN SCHOOL?

"Wow," Jack and I murmured in unison once we'd finished reading.

"I know, right?" said Jenny as she grabbed my hand and steered us to the stairwell that led to the basement, where music was held. We sprinted down the stairs, propelled by our intense curiosity. Who was this lady who had starred in *all* her musicals? I was stabbed by another pang of guilt as I thought how much more excited I was already about this Belinda person than I ever was about Mrs. Wagner. She had never claimed to be the star of anything, except maybe the star of putting kids in a straight line.

As we neared the basement I heard a familiar tune being played on the piano below us. Jack clearly heard it, too, because he stopped abruptly.

"Is that . . . *A Chorus Line*?" he asked.

Sure enough, composer Marvin Hamlisch's iconic intro came wafting up the stairwell.

All of a sudden a woman's voice, brassy and strong, began to sing along:

"One
Singular sensation
Every little step she takes . . ."

"That's gotta be her, right?" Jenny asked,

looking at us with anticipation.

"I'm gonna guess yes," said Jack, who followed us hastily down the stairs, close on our heels. The music grew louder as we turned into the classroom to find Mr. Hennessy sitting at his usual post at the piano. Whereas normally he'd be talking to Mrs. Wagner about local politics or that morning's traffic, he was now plunking out a classic show tune for what could only have been Belinda Grier: a tall, imposing figure step-touching in time to the song.

"She walks into a room
And you know she's uncommonly rare,
Very unique, peripatetic, poetic and chic!"

Upon seeing us, Belinda grinned hugely and gave us a wave. We each gave a tentative wave in return, then shyly took our seats in the second row of folding chairs. We were the first kids to arrive, so it felt like we were walking in on someone's private rehearsal. But Belinda didn't seem shy in the least; she turned back to Mr. Hennessy and just kept singing. With her back turned I was able to get a good look at her.

She wore a pair of purple leggings under a black sheer dance skirt, which I followed with my eyes down to black leg warmers she wore scrunched around her ankles and black booties that peeked out from underneath. On top she wore an off-the-shoulder gray sweater, revealing heavily freckled shoulders. Complementing the freckles was a totally wild mane of curly red hair that Belinda had swept inexplicably into a messy updo—there was so much hair I couldn't see what was keeping it off her neck. She could have had hundreds of bobby pins stuck in there, and I never would have been able to find one. Her ears featured two dangly, spangly earrings which looked more like fishing lures than jewelry. When she turned back around, I noticed that each eye was heavily shadowed with the same purple color as her leggings.

The rest of our classmates were straggling in as Belinda reached the song's big finish:

"She's the,
She's the,
SHE'S THE ONE!"

There was an awkward pause as each person in the class debated silently whether to applaud, but we didn't have to think about it for too long because she beat us to it—she just started clapping for herself, laughing and hooting at Mr. Hennessy, "Woo-hoo! I haven't sung that in forever! Great job, Frank!"

Mr. Hennessy smiled weakly and shifted uncomfortably in his seat—no one, not even Mrs. Wagner, called him by his first name. In fact, I didn't know it was Frank until this moment.

The bell signaling the start of the period rang, and Belinda scanned the room, taking us all in with her big green eyes.

"Hi hi hi, good *morning*, guys!" she said, placing her hands on her hips and assuming a wide stance. She looked like a Jazzercise version of Peter Pan.

"My name is Belinda Grier—please do call me Belinda—and it is so exciting to be on my home turf again. I"—here she paused, drew in her breath, and looked around the room as if she were seeing something that was no longer there—"I haven't been back here in a really long time."

-JACK-

Belinda Grier stood before us like a Radio City Rockette, or rather, the kooky mom of a Rockette. Her presence was remarkable, the type you'd feel even with your eyes closed. Though probably a few years older, she reminded me of the women I'd worked with on Broadway, the kind you could tell were dancers just by the way they stood in line at Starbucks.

"As you've likely heard," Belinda began in a scratchy but strong alto voice, "your teacher Mrs. Wagner has suffered an injury that has unfortunately sidelined her from directing the school musical."

Hilary nodded purposefully from the front row.

"As you've *also* likely heard," Belinda continued, a smile beginning to form on her face, "I, myself hail from Shaker Heights and am even an alumna of this very school." She shifted her weight, bending her knee and pointing her foot in a perfect fourth position.

"Now, before we get down to business," she said, dropping her voice to a warm hum, "I have to tell you, I'm so happy to be back. Everyone knows New York is where it's at, but there really is no place like home."

Lou's eyes snapped over to mine.

"New York," she whispered. "She's from New York, too. You sure you don't know her?"

"Lou," I whispered, rolling my eyes, "I don't know *everyone* in New York."

"Now, I know what you're thinking," Belinda said, straightening her dance skirt. "What would make a working actress leave the glitz and glamour of New York to direct a show at a middle school?"

I don't know, I thought to myself. *Did your voice change? Did you get fired from a Broadway show?* I bet Belinda's story wasn't half as awkward as mine.

"Well." She paused dramatically. She gave her

knuckles a little crack and then shook out her hands. "Well, the short answer is that I happen to have a very special connection to the show that you kids are putting on this spring."

I pushed my elbow into Lou's arm. She pushed back. *Connection? What connection?*

"Now I hate to date myself," she said, looking back at Mr. Hennessy and laughing. "But I was actually *in* the '92 Broadway revival of *Guys and Dolls.*"

Lou's mouth fell open like a nutcracker's. Mr. Mistoffelees crashing through the ceiling and sliding down on a rope would have been less surprising than the news that our director was not only a Broadway actress but had actually been in the acclaimed revival of *Guys and Dolls*. Lou's reaction didn't go unnoticed. Belinda looked over and gave a knowing smile.

"It's true." She winked. Lou blushed.

"For those of you who aren't familiar with the show, let me tell you a little bit about it."

Belinda launched into a detailed description: its plot, the cast of characters, the time period of the piece. Suddenly the musical I'd scoffed at in New York began to seem a whole lot cooler. Sure, it wasn't new or edgy, but there was a reason every theater kept coming back to it—the show was practically perfect. As Belinda continued talking about the musical style and crafty lyrics of Frank Loesser, my mind wandered off to my first encounter with a classic Broadway musical.

Third grade was a big year for me. After the discovery of *Into the Woods* during a fateful trip to the library, I decided to learn everything there was to know about musical theater. I began with the music. Each Friday I'd trot with my dad past the fountains of Lincoln Center to check out a handful of Broadway cast albums from the library, five at a time in alphabetical order.

A Chorus Line, A Class Act, A ... My Name Is Alice, Aida, Annie.

In just a few months I had worked my way up to the Gs, my backpack heavy with scratched cases containing music from *George M!, Gigi, Grey Gardens, Gypsy*, and the 1992 revival of *Guys and Dolls*.

I remember popping the silver disc into my mom's laptop, lying on my stomach as three men with exaggerated New York accents began singing about a horse with the unlikely name of Paul Revere. Although I'd lived in New York, no one sounded as cartoony as these guys. My finger hovered over the eject button as I wondered if any of the other albums had bigger, splashier opening numbers that didn't require a knowledge of Revolutionary War figures. But I was stopped short when my dad popped his head into my room.

"*Guys and Dolls*, right?" he said with a twinkle in his eye.

"Uh, yeah." I looked up, unable to believe my father (a man who enjoyed bird-watching and TV specials about chair making) had known a musical that I didn't.

"Oh, the movie's a classic," he said. "Marlon Brando, Frank Sinatra, that song about rocking the boat, something about a milkshake . . ." He drifted off, his eyes glazing over nostalgically.

"Huh," I mumbled. My finger edged slowly away from the eject button and over to the one that controlled the volume.

"*Luck be a lady tooooo-night*," my dad crooned, walking down the hallway to the kitchen.

Almost instantly, I began hearing the show with a new set of ears. A character named Adelaide sang a song called "A Bushel and a Peck." She was really funny and sounded like she had a clothespin squeezing her nose shut. Another highlight was a song called "Sue Me" that she sang with her fiancé, a guy called Nathan Detroit, a very cool name. While a lot of lyrics confused me, namely references to "sheep's eyes" and "licorice teeth," the melodies were catchy and beautiful, and once my dad explained that the guys singing about horses were in fact criminal gamblers, I was totally hooked.

"At its heart, *Guys and Dolls* is really a love letter to New York City." Belinda's voice fluttered back into my ears, snapping me to attention. I looked around the room. The faces of my classmates bore a wide range of expressions; Jenny: intrigue, Tanner: utter boredom, and of course Lou: in absolute bliss.

"I've had a long, long journey," Belinda said, waltzing over to the piano. "Broadway, national tours, a commercial for Twizzlers . . . But it all began right here in my beloved Shaker Heights," she said, draping her arms across it like a lounge singer.

"Frank remembers, dontcha, Frank?" She

winked at Mr. Hennessy, who shot up on his bench like he'd just had an ice cube dropped down the back of his shirt.

"It was right after graduating from Shaker Heights High that I first auditioned for the show," Belinda said, strutting back to the center of the room. "They didn't cast me at first, but I worked really hard and took a lot of classes so when a new role opened up, I made sure they couldn't resist me." She grinned. "And now to have the opportunity to return home and share all my experience with you. Well, it's just," she said, placing a ruby-nailed hand to her heart, "it feels like destiny."

The way she spoke made me wonder if she'd rehearsed this at home. She sounded like she was in a nightclub doing her one-woman show, not a middle-school classroom in the basement. I half expected Mr. Hennessy to start playing the intro to "Maybe This Time" from *Cabaret*.

"You know, it's crazy," Belinda said. "I haven't been back to Ohio in years. And if I hadn't run into an old friend over the holidays, I'd have never even known you were in such desperate need of a director." She tucked a stray copper ringlet into her nest of hair. "Sometimes the stars they do align."

It really did seem like a crazy coincidence. In fact, everything that had occurred over the holidays seemed to be happening for some strange reason. The fact that I'd run into Corey in a city of eight million, the fact that Mrs. Wagner ended up in a body cast right after Lou and I wished for a better director, "it all seemed," to quote Adelaide, "a horrible dream." And all the more horrible was the fact that deep down, I knew I was happy with the way things were turning out.

Suddenly the sound of the bell vibrated through the room, startling Belinda, who gave a little hop. "Oh, is it time for lunch already? I'm so used to being in a rehearsal room. This being back in school is going to take some getting used to." She giggled through the sounds of scraping chair legs. "I'm also going to be substitute teaching, so if you see me in the hallways, throw me a wave," she said as students began pushing past her.

"Oh, and look for the audition sign-up sheets tomorrow!"

"We *have* to say hi to her," Lou demanded, not even waiting for a response before grabbing my arm and dragging me over to Belinda's desk. As the classroom emptied, Lou and I approached.

"Hi, Ms. Grier."

"Well, hello there," she said, looking up. "And darlin', please, call me Belinda."

"Right," Lou said perkily. "Hi, Belinda. We're Jack and Lou, and we just wanted to give you an official welcome."

"Oh," she tittered. "Well, aren't you the sweetest. I hope you two plan on auditioning for my show next week."

"Oh, we definitely are," Lou fired back. "We're kind of the resident theater nerds around here, so we figured we'd introduce ourselves."

"Well, it's a pleasure to meet you," she said, holding out a long, pale arm, giving our hands a little squeeze. I nodded, taking a step toward the door, but was stopped by the sound of Lou's voice.

"Also, I just wanted to say how cool it is to have a director who's been on Broadway!"

"Oh, why thank you, darlin'," Belinda said, tilting her head.

"We were just in New York last week and got to see a bunch of stuff," Lou continued. "So that 'stars aligning' thing you were talking about, we totally get that."

A tiny "aw" escaped from Belinda's lips.

I looked down at the floor, trying not to groan as Lou laid it on thick. I must not have done a very good job because when I looked back up, Belinda was staring at me, squinting.

"Yes, totally!"

"He speaks!" Belinda cheered, raising her hands in the air.

I laughed awkwardly, leaning my shoulder up against Lou's, hoping she'd take the cue and leave this poor woman alone to enjoy her lunch in peace.

"Also, Jack's been on Broadway, too!" Lou blurted out.

Suddenly the sweet look on Belinda's face disappeared.

"You have?" Her voice dropped.

A wave of embarrassment rushed through me. Lou still hadn't figured out that this stuff made me uncomfortable. I knew she bragged because she was proud, but that kind of excitement wasn't always polite.

"Well, how wonderful!" Belinda clapped her hands together, the warm smile returning. "Two gypsies in one school district. Imagine that!"

"Yeah, he was in *Mary Poppins* and *A Christmas*

Story," Lou said, looking over at me.

Oh boy.

"No kidding." Belinda wrinkled her forehead.

"Yeah," I muttered. "I was a lot younger, though."

"Oh, please," Lou teased. "Jack's just being modest. He was the lead in both of those shows. He's pretty much the Best of Broadway."

"Ha!" I laughed uncomfortably, elbowing Lou. "She's definitely exaggerating, but hey, that's cool that we've both been on Broadway," I said hurriedly. "We probably know some of the same people."

"I bet you're right," Belinda said. "What's your last name, Jack?"

"Uh, Goodrich," I replied. "Jack Goodrich."

Her eyes flashed. "Oh," she said with boosted interest. "I think I know who you are."

I bit the inside of my cheek.

"We're going to have *all kinds* of things to talk about," she said, crossing her arms.

I looked over at Lou, but she just stood there, grinning. She probably couldn't believe her luck that in the past week her number of Broadway pals had somehow quadrupled.

"Well," Belinda said, breaking from our little triangle. "It was so nice meeting you two." She began packing up her purse. "I can tell this is going to be so fun! Oh, and Jack," she said throwing me a sideways glance, "I look forward to trading some war stories."

Seven

-LOUISA-

"Way to embarrass me, Lou," Jack grumbled as we ascended the stairs to the first floor.

"What are you talking about?" I asked in a shocked voice. "How did I embarrass you?"

"Oh, I don't know," he said sarcastically, "maybe by giving Belinda my entire resume?!"

"Oh, c'mon," I said, "she already knows who you are; she said so herself!"

Jack snorted.

"You certainly gave her enough clues to figure that out."

"She would have figured it out eventually," I countered, "and just think—now that she knows you're, like, the real deal, she's more likely to give you whatever part you want!"

"Ugh, you're worse than my mom."

I ignored his dig and began to sing the title song of *Guys and Dolls*:

"When you see a guy
Reach for stars in the sky . . ."

I bounded up the remaining stairs, my voice bouncing off the concrete walls and making Jack cover his ears.

"Okay, I get it, you're excited, Lou!" he shouted, trying to quiet me.

"Excited?!" I squealed. "Excited is an understatement. I'm . . . *ecstatic*."

Meeting Belinda Grier had left me feeling giddy. I let out another squeal, thinking about how Belinda was living proof that a girl from Shaker Heights could make it on Broadway. I burst through the double doors into the first-floor hallway, launching into "Adelaide's Lament":

"The average unmarried female,
Basically insecure . . ."

The first time I'd ever heard "Adelaide's Lament"

was at a restaurant on Cape Cod that featured singing waiters and waitresses. I was eight years old, and as the song began my mom whispered in my ear, "Oh, I love this one." By the time the number was over, I loved it, too—so much so that I forced my mom out of her beach chair the next day so we could search stores for the cast album. There are a few recordings of *Guys and Dolls*, but the one I chose was the celebrated 1992 version starring Nathan Lane, Faith Prince, Peter Gallagher, and Josie de Guzman—the same production that Belinda Grier had joined later in its run. I listened to it nonstop for weeks, mimicking Faith Prince's hysterical squeaks and her nasal delivery of lines like, "*Nathan*. This is the *biggest* lie you've ever *told* me!" I knew that I had to play Adelaide someday. Maybe—hopefully— that day was coming soon.

"What are you doing *now*?" Jack said as he caught up to me.

"Huh?" I said, startled.

"You're muttering to yourself, but in a weird voice. Like an old-fashioned telephone operator."

As he tried to replicate the sounds I'd been making, I blushed, realizing what I must have been doing. It didn't take long for Jack to figure it out, either.

"Wait . . . are you already working on Adelaide's *lines?*" He started to laugh. "You don't even know which sides Belinda will pick for the audition!"

"Whatever, I was just reminding myself . . ."

"*Uh-huh.*"

"Oh, like you're not gonna go home and YouTube 'Nathan Detroit *Guys and Dolls*' later."

"Maybe I don't want to play Nathan Detroit," Jack replied coyly. "I mean, Nicely-Nicely Johnson is a pretty great part, too."

He was right—Nicely-Nicely, who's kind of Nathan's right-hand man, was another great part, and Jack would do a great job with it. But in my fantasy, we'd play Nathan and Adelaide. That would just be perfect.

Much to my chagrin, Jack was reading my mind.

"Me playing Nicely-Nicely isn't part of your 'master plan,' is it?" He teased, "You're already designing our Nathan and Adelaide costumes, aren't you?"

Embarrassed, I elbowed Jack in the ribs.

"I knew it!" He laughed triumphantly.

"Whatever—you were thinking it, too!"

"Yeah, but in a 'Wouldn't that be cool if' kind of way. You're, like, staging our curtain call already." I clenched my fist, ready to go with my elbow again, but Jack ran ahead of me to avoid a second jab. Rounding the corner into another hallway, he nearly collided with Coach Wilson, whose soccer tryouts Jack had escaped to audition for *Into the Woods.*

"Whoa, there," he said, lifting up his hands, which each held a full cup of coffee.

"Oops, sorry, Coach Wilson," mumbled Jack. It was his turn to be embarrassed. I smiled, feeling smug.

"That could have been pretty messy, huh?" Coach Wilson said, though he didn't seem angry. In fact, he seemed pretty happy. Maybe it was because he was about to drink two cups of coffee. Adults were weirdly enthusiastic about their coffee.

"Where are you two coming from?"

"Music," I replied, relishing my role as the good student who didn't run carelessly in the halls.

"Oh! So you met Belinda!" he exclaimed happily.

"Yeah, we did," confirmed Jack.

"It's real exciting that she's back," said Coach Wilson, beaming. "When she was in school here, she was the talk of the town. Everybody knew that girl was going places."

"Yeah," said Jack, a mischievous glint in his eye, "sounds like she hasn't been back here *in a really long time.*"

I shot him a look.

"I'll admit I'm surprised to see her," confirmed Coach Wilson, "but it sure is a *pleasant* surprise."

"Yeah, we're psyched," I said. "She seems really neat."

"She *is* neat," Coach Wilson said, nodding. He looked down at his two coffee cups, then back at us. I wasn't sure if we were supposed to say more, so I just smiled and nodded back. I guess that was enough for Coach Wilson, because he went on, "You know, it's terrible news about Mrs. Wagner. But she's a tough ole gal; she'll pull through just fine. In the meantime . . ." He paused, as if searching for the right way to be sympathetic but also optimistic. "In the meantime, you kids are in for quite a treat!" Winking at us, he turned around and headed toward the double doors we'd walked through moments before.

The rest of the school day dragged on as teachers outlined their remaining curriculum with about as much enthusiasm as I had for gym class.

"Civil War leading into Reconstruction . . ."

"Positive and negative integers . . ."

"The ecology surrounding the Great Lakes . . ."

"Homework for tonight . . ."

"Homework for the week . . ."

"Homework for the month . . ."

Needless to say, I raced to catch the bus as soon as the final bell rang. Jack, Jenny, and I had some homework of our own that demanded our immediate attention.

"She said it feels like 'destiny'?" Jenny's mom asked once we'd relayed Belinda's introductory speech. "She really said that?"

We were gathered around the Westcotts' kitchen table, ready to interrogate Jenny's mom about Belinda Grier as we nibbled on snacks she'd laid out.

"Uh-huh," said Jenny, reaching for an apple slice and popping it into her mouth. "She talked about the stars aligning."

"That is so surprising to me," Mrs. Westcott said. "I didn't think she'd ever come back; I mean, she hasn't been back in a really long time."

Jack and I exchanged a look, trying not to giggle.

"So," I ventured, "what was Belinda like when you knew her?"

"Determined," Mrs. Westcott said without hesitation. "Incredibly confident. A force of nature, really. She just knew what she wanted and wasn't going to let anything stand in her way. Oh, and she had legs that went on for days."

"She still does," said Jenny. "I can tell her turnout is amazing."

"She also has a perfect bevel," added Jack.

"Totally," I chimed in. "Her overall posture is just fantas—"

"*Wait!*"

Mrs. Westcott's hands suddenly slammed down on the table, making Jack drop the pita chip he was about to dip into a container of hummus.

Mrs. Westcott leaped from her chair and ran out of the kitchen and up the stairs. Jenny, Jack, and I exchanged confused glances as we heard a thud above us.

"It sounds like she's digging around in her closet," Jenny guessed. Moments later, we heard Mrs. Westcott's muffled "Found it!" followed by the soft thumps of her footsteps on the carpeted stairs. Breathing hard, she appeared back in the kitchen holding a black VHS tape. "I knew I hadn't thrown this away," she gasped. "This is our high-school production of *Once Upon a Mattress*. Belinda and I were both seniors. She played the lead. You wanna pop it in and take a look?"

I wasn't sure what was more astonishing— that Jenny's mom had been able to find the tape so quickly or that her family *still owned a VCR*— but the answer to Mrs. Westcott's question was a definite yes.

The quality of the tape was pretty poor. The camera kept wobbling and the sound was uneven, but one thing was unmistakable: Belinda Grier was indeed a force of nature. With her long, thin legs, curly red mane, and brassy voice, Belinda stood out in a sea of shuffling, out-of-tune teenagers. They were doing a production of *Once Upon a Mattress*, which is a musical retelling of *The Princess and the Pea*, and the lead character of Princess Winnifred is a loud, unapologetic, lovable goof who captures the heart of Prince Dauntless much to the dismay of his mother, the Queen. Leaning forward on the Westcotts' couch, Jack, Jenny, and I watched in wonder as Belinda nailed every joke, sailed through every note, and mastered every dance step.

"She's incredible," I said, mesmerized.

Jack and Jenny nodded in unison.

"Fierce," said Jenny.

"Stupid fierce," said Jack.

"See if you can find *me!*" Mrs. Westcott stood behind the couch, watching over our heads. Jenny hopped off the couch and scooted on her knees toward the television screen, peering closely. She pointed to one of the dozen ladies-in-waiting, standing in a clump upstage.

"Is that you, Mom?" Jenny asked.

"That's me, Lady-in-Waiting Number Seven." Mrs. Westcott laughed. "I did the musical more for social reasons, not for stardom."

"Why does *that* kid look familiar?" Jenny asked, squinting even more closely at the screen. Both

Jack and I joined Jenny on the floor to see who she
was talking about, and we followed her pointing
finger to the lanky boy playing Prince Dauntless.
He came nowhere near the level of Belinda's
talent, but there was something charming about
him—mostly because he seemed to be having a lot
of fun onstage. And Jenny was right—there was
something oddly familiar about him. I turned to
see Mrs. Westcott giggling.

"He should look familiar," she said, grinning,
"though he's filled out a bit since 1991."

We inched even closer to the screen. Jack let out
a small gasp.

"Oh my God," he whispered, "it's Coach Wilson."

Jenny and I squealed.

"Oh my God, it *is* Coach Wilson!" Jenny
screamed. "Look at how *skinny* he was!"

"Well, back then he was Mike Wilson," Mrs.
Westcott corrected, "and he was our star soccer
player. But he got hurt during practice early in our
senior year, so he had to sit out the season. In high
school they do the musical in the fall, so our drama
director recruited him for *Once Upon a Mattress*."

We stared at Jenny's mom, our mouths agape.

"I have to say," she said, "he started out really

shy in rehearsals, but by the time we opened he'd turned into quite the ham."

As if to illustrate Mrs. Westcott's point, we heard a shriek from the television screen, only to catch Coach—I mean, Mike—Wilson executing a pretty decent pratfall, his gangly limbs flailing.

"I think Belinda brought out his inner clown," Jenny's mom continued, "or forced it out, really. She wanted to look good on that stage, you know? So she worked with him a lot to make sure her leading man was up to snuff." Suddenly our run-in with Coach Wilson earlier that day took on a whole new meaning.

"You kids are in for quite a treat!" he'd said, then headed toward the double doors leading to the basement stairwell, carrying two cups of coffee. One of those cups must have been for Belinda, who did mention that she'd run into "an old friend over the holidays." Watching the two of them in *Once Upon a Mattress* made it clear why he was so excited—his leading lady had returned home.

"Well, I'm psyched," declared Jenny, hitting the pause button on the VCR. "Belinda seems awesome."

I looked at Jack, who sat nodding enthusiastically in agreement.

I suddenly had an image of poor Mrs. Wagner laid up in a hospital bed, encased in a body cast. I felt bad that no one, not Coach Wilson, not Mrs. Westcott, and certainly not Jack, Jenny, or me, seemed too upset that she'd been replaced. But I felt good knowing that we would probably not be standing in a straight line anytime soon. Not with Belinda Grier running the show.

-JACK-

"Have you memorized your lines yet?" Lou asked the next day, slamming her locker shut.

"What are you talking about?" I laughed. "Belinda hasn't even announced what scenes we're doing for the auditions yet!"

"Right," Lou said, slinging her backpack over her shoulder. "But I've narrowed it down to the scenes before 'Sue Me' and 'Marry the Man Today.' They show off both dramatic and comedic range and only have two people in each scene, making them prime audition options," she said, following me to homeroom. "I figured I'd look at them both; that way no matter what she chooses, I'll have a head start."

We walked down the hallway past the nurse's office and the giant trophy case. As we turned the corner we were met with a vision of Belinda perched on a ladder, a roll of tape around her wrist, plastering audition posters to the wall.

"Well," I whispered to Lou, "why don't you just ask her yourself?"

Even while taping up posters, Belinda seemed to be striking a pose. She wore a pair of leopard-print leggings, a bright orange top, and a cropped leather jacket. Her shoes, I recognized immediately as LaDucas, a fancy brand of dance heel often worn by Broadway chorus girls. Her knee was bent, her foot pointing out like someone being kissed in a 1940s romantic comedy.

"Well, if it isn't my little minions," Belinda said, throwing us a wily smile.

"Hey, Belinda," we sang in unison.

"I'm just finishing up with these audition announcements," she said, slinking down the ladder. "What do you think?"

The wall was plastered floor to ceiling with rows of brightly colored paper. It looked like a downtown Manhattan construction site, the kind always lined with band posters.

"They look awesome," I said enthusiastically.

"Speaking of which," Lou cut in sneakily, "do you have any idea what the audition material for Nathan and Adelaide is going to be?"

"Oh, so you've decided to go for the comic duo rather than the pair of ingénues," Belinda said, lifting her chin. "Wise choice. And, yes, I do have an idea, but you'll have to wait until music class to find out."

"You got it," Lou cheeped, her disappointment well hidden. "Oh!" she blurted, causing all of us to jump a little. "You're never gonna believe this! My other best friend, Jenny, she's a ballerina actually, but that's not the point. The point is, Jenny's mom went to school with you and was actually in your senior year musical!"

Belinda gasped. "*Once Upon a Mattress*," she said, a proud look taking over her face.

"Yeah," Lou continued. "And Jenny's mom still had a recording of the production and showed it to us, and omigosh"—Lou sighed—"you were so amazing."

"You really were," I added truthfully.

"You know, they pretty much chose that show for me," Belinda said, gliding up to us like a kid eyeing the last slice of birthday cake. "See, I played Bianca in *Kiss Me, Kate* my sophomore year, so everyone assumed I was just a dancer, but then I surprised them all by getting Audrey in *Little Shop of Horrors* the next year. See, I could do comedy, too," she said, nodding eagerly. "So when they announced *Mattress*, it was pretty much understood that I'd be playing Winnifred."

I could tell Belinda was an authority on many things, but her biggest area of expertise was, without a doubt, Belinda.

"Well, you were awesome." I smiled.

"What's your friend's mom's name?" Belinda asked, looking over at Lou.

"Um, it's Amy. Amy Westcott." Lou shrugged. "But that's her married name. I'm not sure what her last name was in high school."

"*Amy Westcott*," Belinda whispered to herself. I waited for a flicker of recognition to sputter in her eyes, but none did.

"Really pretty. Long black hair. She was a Lady-in-Waiting," Lou added. "Number seven, I think."

"Number *seven*?! How many of them were there?!" Belinda said with a chuckle. "Hmm, no. Don't think I can place her."

"Well . . . ," Lou said. "I'm working on getting her daughter Jenny to audition. Like I said, she's a ballerina. In fact, *a lot* of girls from our class said they're going to be at tryouts next Thursday."

Belinda nodded, pleased.

"The real challenge is going to be finding boys," Lou continued. "Of course Jack will be there, but I haven't really heard of any other guys who are planning on auditioning."

Belinda remained silent for a moment, staring Lou right in the eye. I wondered if she'd made a mistake by opening her mouth. Belinda didn't seem like a person who enjoyed getting bad news.

"Worst-case scenario," I butted in. "You could just dress up some of the eighth-grade girls in baggy suits," I tried to joke. "Or change the title to *Dolls*."

But my words were cut short as the force of something smacked me in the back, forcing me to crash into Lou. I looked down to find a soccer ball rolling past my feet. I traced its path back up the hallway to a cluster of boys.

"Whoops, sorry, dude," a voice shouted, amid a chorus of snickers. I recognized it immediately as Tanner Falzone's.

"My bad," he said, giggling. "I was aiming for Sebastian." Sebastian Maroney was the goalie of the soccer team, a kid who at twelve years of age had a deeper voice than my dad's. The two swaggered down the hall, followed by a pack of boys wearing nylon warm-ups and hiding their laughter behind their hands. Lou reached down and scooped up the ball.

"Well, if that's how you aim," she said, squeezing the ball, her knuckles beginning to turn white as she scowled at Tanner, "it's no wonder you guys got creamed at the championship game."

"OHHHHHHHH!" the boys wailed, pointing frenzied fingers at Tanner. This was apparently even funnier than pelting the theater geeks with a soccer ball.

"Yeah . . . well," Tanner said, suddenly red in the face. "Well, maybe *you* should practice some more high notes!"

"OHHHHHHHH!" the boys echoed robotically, pointing at Lou, although with less gusto. Their faces looked more confused than anything.

"Hey, good one, guys," I said, grabbing the ball out of Lou's hands, trying to defuse the situation. "Here ya go."

I bounced it off my knee and straight into Sebastian's waiting hands. This, for some reason, made the team giggle even more. Last semester, these boys were my main source of anxiety. Now, I had nothing to hide, but I still went to great lengths to cover up the fact that they pretty much terrified me.

"Come on, guys," Tanner said, cocking his head to his teammates.

Like a well-trained army, they filed into a line and brushed past us. Just as they rounded the corner Belinda leaned in and whispered sharply, "What about those boys?"

Lou and I looked to each other, confused.

"Those boys could be my gangsters," Belinda said urgently.

"Your what?!" I spit out, sounding slightly more shocked than intended.

"My gangsters in the show!" she exclaimed. "Harry the Horse, Angie the Ox, Big Jule. Look at them! They're perfect."

I jerked my head over toward Lou, who just stood there, blinking.

"Those guys," I said, pointing down the hallway, "do *not* do musicals. Trust me."

"Why not?" Belinda said, suddenly taken aback. "It's thirty-two degrees outside. Soccer season doesn't start for a few months."

"Yeah, but—" Lou tried to interject.

"They play soccer, so I already know they can kick," Belinda went on. "A couple of bar stretches and they'll be in tip-top shape to learn the Crapshooters' Ballet."

"Ballet?!" I cried, shaking my head. "The day the soccer team does ballet is the day that Lake Superior freezes over."

"Lake Superior freezes over as a polar vortex sweeps through the Midwest," the radio weatherman announced as I scarfed down my bowl of granola. "Reaching a full one hundred percent freeze rate for the first time since 1979, residents of Michigan, Ohio, and Indiana are advised to avoid prolonged exposure to the outdoors until the thermometer climbs back up into the double digits."

"Are you ready for the dance call today?" my mom asked, looking up from the lunch bag she'd been packing me.

"I guess so," I said, swallowing. "I might be the only guy who shows up, so even if I fall on my face, I don't think it will hurt my chances."

"Well, try not to do that," my dad said, entering the kitchen. "Make sure you warm up first. It's cold days like these that you're most likely to injure yourself."

"I know, Dad," I said with a sigh, spooning up the last bit of almond milk from my bowl. "I just hope I'm not alone up there."

"Thank you for showing up today," Belinda said, pacing across the stage looking out into the audience of nervous auditioners. The final ring of the school bell had cued nearly thirty students to pour into the auditorium, an impressive number by Shaker Heights standards, Lou was quick to point out. The only boys I saw were Garett Kirsch (a short boy from my homeroom), Travis Nordin (a skinny eighth-grader), and one boy I didn't recognize from the sixth grade. Normally I'd be relieved, knowing my chances of getting Nathan Detroit were much better, but with only four guys to fill an entire cast, was this even a show I wanted to be a part of?

"We'll be breaking up the audition over the course of two days. Tomorrow will be the acting and singing portion. Today will be the dance call," Belinda said, holding up a clipboard. "I'm going to give you numbers to pin to the front of your shirt or leotard. Make sure they are visible."

"Old-school," I whispered to Lou.

"We'll begin with the girls." As she spoke she began stretching various parts of her body. Her green leg warmers bobbed with each *plié*. "Hopefully more boys will show up, but in the meantime, I'll be teaching eight counts of eight to 'Take Back Your Mink.' I realize that not all of you are at the same level, but try your hardest and remember," she said, rolling her ankle in a circle, "there's always next year. Now, when I call your name, please come to the stage to get your number. *Danielle Abbott, Nina Avalon . . .*"

The dance combination whizzed by. The steps were unusually difficult, even for the girls I'd seen cheerleading on the pep squad.

"Fan kick, three, four, fan kick, seven, eight," Belinda called out, her leg swinging past her ears like windshield wipers.

"*Chaînés*, two, three, four, pivot step, seven, pose!"

The majority of the girls struggled, looking like marionettes with their strings tangled, jerking their limbs seemingly at random. Lou, who I'd never seen dance before, looked somewhat shell-shocked. It was impossible not to notice that she was hitting many of the poses on the wrong counts. The only person who seemed to be keeping up was Jenny, the trained ballerina.

"All right, now that we've all learned the steps," Belinda said abruptly, not even the slightest bit out of breath, "let's take a quick five. Afterward I'll be breaking you up into smaller groups to audition for me."

The girls slogged to the wings, grasping for water bottles and towels. Lou, desperate for help, ran up to Jenny, who was still onstage stretching. I watched as they began marking through the movement, Lou trying to keep up, obviously still confused.

"Lou, your feet should be *ouverte* to start. And the balance is *devant*. You're doing it *derrière*."

"Ooo-what?"

Lou tried to take her corrections, but I could see

Jenny's dance expertise was only making things
more complicated. Sometimes the best dancers
are the worst teachers. As Jenny continued to
talk about her *port de bras* and *aplomb*, Lou stood,
flustered, rubbing the back of her head with her
hand. I could tell she wasn't getting it.

"Excuse me," I said, leaping to my feet and
scooting past Travis in my row.

"*Lou*," I whispered, charging down the aisle.

She looked up, her eyes filled with panic. I
flicked my head to the right, signaling to a corner
free of girls and dance bags. She looked back at
Jenny, who shrugged and gestured for her to
join me.

"I know. I'm a mess," Lou huffed anxiously as
she clopped down the stairs. "Adelaide's supposed
to dance front and center. There's no way she's
going to cast me if I can't even remember the steps."

"You're fine," I said, placing my hand on her
shoulder. "Just breathe. You look great. I just think
Belinda's counts are confusing you."

"Is the first arm throw on the four or the five?"
Lou asked hurriedly.

"It's on the five, but maybe try not to think of
it like that," I said calmly. "Mr. Hennessy is playing

the accompaniment to the song, right? I know you know all the words, so if you sing along quietly, the dance steps will make way more sense."

"Okay," Lou said, nodding quickly.

"*Take back your MINK*," I said, cycling through the first phrase. "The arm throw is actually on the word *mink*, which makes total sense if you think about it, like she's throwing off her coat."

Lou mouthed the words and walked through the movement, this time throwing her arm in the right place.

"And I think you've been putting that shimmy on the wrong count," I said, moving on to another section. "Lyrically it lines up with, '*It all seems a HORRIBLE dream.*'"

"You're right!" Lou exclaimed.

After giving her a few more pointers, I said, "Even if you mess up, it's just an audition. Belinda knows you'll have weeks to perfect it. Just show her that you can make some bold choices."

"And we're back," Belinda's voice blared through the auditorium.

I looked over to find her staring directly as us. I don't know why, but something in her eyes made me think we'd been caught doing something we weren't supposed to.

"Thanks, Jack," Lou whispered. I could tell she was still nervous.

I gave her shoulder a final squeeze. "You got this."

I watched nervously as Belinda broke up the girls into groups of four. The first few were shaky, mistaking right arms for left and pivots for ball changes, but as the numbers grew higher, the groups seemed to improve. The girls began hitting the right marks and looking more confident. By the time she reached Jenny's group, they were not only dancing cleanly but infusing the movement with character.

"Numbers twenty-one, twenty-two, twenty-three, and twenty-four," Belinda called out.

Twenty-three was Lou's number. She made her way to the downstage right position, hands on her hips and a saccharine smile pinned across her face. As Mr. Hennessy began the intro, Jenny threw her a final thumbs-up from the sidelines. Once the combination began it was as though a spotlight had beamed down from the rafters, shining directly on Lou. The girls lining the wings halted their nervous fidgeting to watch as she danced. She made hilarious faces and accented beats with *Oohs* and *Woos* like we'd seen the speakeasy girls do in *Let's Make a Toast!* While her kicks weren't as high and her short frame perhaps not as "dancer-like" as some of the other girls, she more than made up for it with her plucky charm. As the final count of eight began, Lou jumped a step, mistaking a *chassé* for a turn. Belinda winced, yet Lou seemed to act as if it were nothing, instead replacing the missed counts with a spontaneous ad-lib.

"Nathan, look whatcha made me do!" she whined in her best, most nasally Adelaide voice. Everyone, including Belinda, burst into laughter. I was so proud.

"Thank you, ladies," she said as the final group buttoned the number. "You may take your seats."

As the girls trotted down the stairs, Belinda walked center stage and placed her hands over her eyes like a visor, scanning the audience. I reached my hand out and gave a high five to Lou, who was now squeezing into my row. A surge of excitement shot through my body. I knew I was up next.

"Hmm," Belinda muttered from downstage.

"I really thought there'd be more boys."

"We tried to warn her," Lou whispered, her wooden chair creaking as she plopped down next to me.

"I might have to rethink . . . ," Belinda mumbled, beginning to pace across the stage. "Gosh, I'm not sure . . . I don't know if it's worth . . ." She checked the silver watch on her wrist and crossed over to Mr. Hennessy at the piano.

I sat up straight in my chair, craning to overhear their conversation. A whisper of panic began spreading through the room.

"She might have to rethink what?" I looked over at Lou.

"I don't know," Lou whispered back.

Belinda's beehive of hair quivered behind the piano as fragments of conversation drifted up and into the room.

"I mean, I can't have girls play every part."

"Do you think we should just . . ."

"The whole thing?"

"Oh no." Lou turned to me with concern. "What's going on?"

"Ladies and gentlemen," Belinda bellowed as she chugged back down to the front of the stage, her face twisted into a frown. "It pains me to announce that the boys' dance call has been canceled."

A flurry of whispers swept through the auditorium.

"And because we only have four boys," she said, speaking over the tumult, "I think we're going to have to—"

But her words were cut short as a screech of steel rang through the back of the auditorium. Thirty heads turned in unison. The big set of doors swung open and twenty pairs of dirty sneakers clomped into the room.

"Did we miss the audition?" a voice called out.

I traced my eyes up the aisle to the sight of Tanner Falzone and Sebastian Maroney, standing with their arms crossed in the doorway. Behind them stood the entire boys' soccer team.

Nine

-LOUISA-

There are things you never expect to see: a whale riding a bicycle, for example, or rain shooting up into the sky instead of pouring down to the ground. But seeing twenty boys from the Shaker Heights Middle School soccer team arrive en masse at an audition for *Guys and Dolls* suddenly made bicycle-riding whales seem like an actual possibility, as their appearance was as unlikely as anything I could have imagined. Yet here they were; I was staring at them with my own eyes—and what made the whole situation even crazier was that they seemed to be *staying*. I didn't need to look at Jack to know that he was equally shocked, but nevertheless, I turned to find him blinking rapidly, as if the image of Tanner and the rest of the boys would disappear after one of those blinks. I noticed that everyone else in the auditorium was staring in disbelief, too. Everyone, that is, except for one very excited redhead.

"Hallelujah!" cried Belinda, throwing her arms in the air and launching into a box step. "My prayers have been answered!" She thrust out her arms and motioned the boys toward the stage.

"Come up, come up, come up!" she called out to them. "All boys onstage now, and start stretching! The dance call is *back on!*"

The soccer boys hesitated, uncertain. But then a familiar voice called out from behind them: "You heard her, guys, up and at 'em."

As the boys obeyed the order and started down the aisle toward the stage, I saw Coach Wilson standing under the Exit sign, arms crossed, smiling broadly.

"*Thank you*, Mike! Oops! I mean, *Coach!*" Belinda shouted from the stage, clasping her hands together and shaking them with gratitude. I looked back at Coach Wilson, who held out his hands toward the soccer boys, palms up, as if to say, "They're all yours."

As shocked as I'd felt seconds earlier at their arrival, I now saw how inevitable all of it was, given Coach and Belinda's shared theatrical history. Of course she would take advantage of their friendship to recruit his players for the school musical; in her shoes, I would have done the same. Still, their presence dramatically changed the energy in the room, making it a little more dangerous and unpredictable.

Coach Wilson gave a slight nod toward Belinda, then exited into the lobby. Belinda called from the stage: "I still see some 'Guys' out there! Get your heinies up here!"

"You better get going," I urged Jack gently. He exhaled loudly.

"This is going to be interesting," he said, and as he scooted past me to get to the aisle, I grabbed his wrist.

"Hey—they're on *your* turf; just remember that."

"Yeah, I don't know if that's a good thing," he said, tugging nervously at his shirt as he made his way toward the stage. Jenny was now climbing out of her seat and scurrying to join me in my row, her face contorted in a grimace.

"Why do I feel like this is going to be painful to watch?" she asked, taking Jack's now-vacated seat. She had practically read my mind. As soon as Jack arrived onstage, Tanner turned to his teammates.

"Oh shoot, guys, I forgot my tights at home— Jack, do you have an extra pair I could borrow?" His crack was greeted by a round of snorts and snickers from the boys around him. My cheeks burned as I willed Jack to make a snappy comeback, but all he did was head toward the back row of boys.

He must have known that such a plan was never going to work, though, not after Belinda had referred to us as her "minions" just days earlier. Sure enough, as soon as all the boys were assembled on the stage, Belinda barked, "Jack! Where'd you go?"

There was a pause, and then a barely audible "Here" rose from behind the clump of tall soccer players.

Belinda, seemingly clueless about the vast differences between jocks and theater nerds, had no patience for Jack's shyness.

"What are you doing *back there*?" she

demanded. "Come up to the front, since you've done this kind of thing *professionally*."

"What is she trying to do?" Jenny whispered. "Guarantee that Jack have no friends for the rest of his life?"

"He'll be okay," I whispered back, though I wasn't entirely convinced he would be. I could see Tanner elbowing Martin Howe and stifling a laugh as Jack walked downstage toward Belinda. Jack kept his eyes down, doing his best to attract as little attention as possible. As he settled on a spot just left of center stage, Belinda turned to face all the girls still sitting in the audience.

"Ladies," she began, "thank you so much for your time today. Come back tomorrow, same time, for the acting and singing call." Jenny and I exchanged a look as the rest of the girls gathered their coats and bags.

"We're staying, aren't we?" she asked, already knowing that I wasn't going to abandon my friend.

"I have to stay—after he saved me in my dance call, the least I can do is be here for him. But you can go," I said. Jenny narrowed her eyes at me.

"Oh, no, I can't. Jack may need you, but you need *me*. Just don't get mad if I have to cover my eyes."

Belinda was already busy assigning numbers to the boys. Upon receiving the number eighteen, Tanner called out happily, "Hey, that's my jersey number! Sweet!"

"It's the little things," deadpanned Jenny, which made me giggle even though I was feeling anxious. Thank goodness she was staying.

"Okay, this is going to be *fun*! I *looove* being back on this stage!" Belinda cheered once she'd made it through all the boys. She rolled her shoulders back and shook out her horselike legs.

"Frank, give me a little 'Luck Be a Lady,' would you?"

Mr. Hennessy, now fully resigned to being called Frank, began to plunk out the melody on the piano. Belinda bounced on the balls of her feet.

"I'll dance through it once, then I'll break it down into sections. Once we've learned each section, we'll put the whole thing together, and then split you up into groups, okay? Okay! *Five, six, seven, eight!*"

As Mr. Hennessy started the song from the beginning, Belinda launched into the dance combination, once again calling out dance terms as she moved: "*Chassé, chassé, chassé*, jump! Pivot

turn, pivot turn. *Chassé, chassé, chassé,* jump!
Pivot turn, pivot turn. *Jeté* left, *jeté* right. Step-
touch, step-touch, *chaînés, chaînés, chaînés,
chaînés...*"

Behind her, the soccer boys watched in
horrified fascination, their faces a perfect blend
of confusion, disbelief, and fear. What made
Belinda think that any of them would be able to
learn this, especially when she was using French
ballet terms that none of them had ever heard
before? I had barely made it through my own
dance combination, and I'd taken a lot of dance
classes in my life! If it hadn't been for Jack's help,
who knows what would have happened.

Oblivious to the baffled boys behind her,
Belinda outdid herself with the last eight counts
of the routine: "Kick ball change, kick ball change,
jump and lunge, REACH!" On the last note of
the music, Belinda, in a deep forward lunge,
thrust her right hand toward the floor as if she
was throwing a pair of dice. I had to admit, the
combination was pretty great. But great for, like,
actual dancers.

"Okay, let's take it from the top—the first
eight counts!" Belinda shouted, slightly out of

breath. "A five, six, seven, eight!"

Only Jack started to follow along. None of the other boys moved. Belinda, already halfway across the stage, stopped and turned around, bewildered by their stillness.

"C'mon, boys," she said, "don't be shy. Five, six, seven—"

"Ahem . . . ?"

Tanner cleared his throat, interrupting Belinda's count off.

"Yes, what is it, Number Eighteen?" asked Belinda. She looked genuinely surprised that someone might have a question.

"Miss, uh . . . ?"

"Belinda. Call me Belinda."

"Belinda . . . We can't do this."

"You can't? Why not?"

"Because—" He started to laugh. "We can't dance. Not like that."

Belinda pursed her lips and inhaled loudly through her nose, a bloom of crimson spreading across her freckled cheeks.

"But you haven't even tried," she said carefully, her voice deepening, "so how do you know if you can or can't?"

Oh no, I thought, *this is where it all falls apart. If Tanner leaves, the rest will follow. That's how it goes. Then Belinda will say she has no interest in doing "Dolls," and we won't have any show at all.* I turned to Jenny, who, sure enough, was now shielding her eyes with her hands. Then I turned to look at Jack, whose eyes were darting back and forth between Belinda and Tanner. I could tell he was thinking something—his face was tense, like he had something to say.

"Yeah, but . . ." Tanner sighed, looking at his teammates, all of them desperate to escape. "We just . . . can't."

As he took a step toward the edge of the stage, signaling to his friends that they should follow, Jack's voice cut through the air: "*It's like soccer.*"

The boys stopped and stared at Jack, who instantly froze under their gaze. Belinda's head jerked in his direction.

"What are you talking about, Jack?" she asked, planting her hands on her hips.

"If you think of the moves like soccer moves," Jack began hesitantly, "then it's not that hard."

"I think if you just watch it a few more times, you'll get the hang of it," Belinda interjected.

"I know I can teach you if you just show a little patien—"

Tanner didn't let her finish.

"Like what kind of soccer moves?" he asked, stepping so close to Jack that Belinda was forced to take a step backward. Jenny peeled her fingers from her eyes.

"What is happening?" she whispered.

"Shh," I said, patting her knee to be quiet. I sat up in my seat and leaned forward, riveted by the unfolding scene onstage. Jack shot me an uneasy glance, and in that split second I nodded back at him reassuringly. He turned to Tanner and began to explain.

"Well, like, a 'fake'—that's like a 'pivot turn' in dance. Think of faking out your opponent by changing directions—that's basically what a pivot turn is." He demonstrated. More boys moved closer to watch. Belinda cocked her head, eyeing Jack with curiosity.

"And, like, when you're moving down the field but you need to keep your eye on the ball, so you're basically, like, galloping sideways? That's like a *chassé*."

Again, Jack demonstrated by moving across the

floor. This time, a few boys followed along—and followed pretty well.

"Okay!" Belinda cheered. "See? It's not that difficult, right? Want to try to put this all together now?"

"Wait," said Tanner, not paying any attention to Belinda, "what about those crazy-fast moves at the end, Jack? How were those like soccer?"

"Oh, the kick ball changes?" said Jack. "Think of kicking the ball straight with your right leg but then having to run to the left."

Tanner mimed kicking a ball and running to the left.

"Exactly! See?" Jack said, pointing to Tanner's feet. "You naturally stepped back on your right foot first, then stepped with your left. Do it a little faster and closer to your body—and that's a kick ball change."

Jenny let out a small gasp. "This is sort of amazing."

She was right—my friend Jack Goodrich, MTN extraordinaire, was teaching twenty soccer players how to dance. He was patient, clear, confident. And no one, not even Tanner Falzone, was laughing at him. No one was making fun of him, and no one seemed to want to leave—they were totally focused.

"This is cool," Martin conceded as he tried out a kick ball change with success.

"Yeah, Jack," Sebastian chimed in, pivot-turning like a pro, "this makes it so much easier—thanks."

I looked across to the other side of the stage, where Belinda now stood, curious to see what she thought of Jack's dance miracle. Her hands were clasped tightly together and her eyes looked kind of wild as she broke into an enormous toothy grin.

"All right, Jack, it looks like they're ready!" she barked, clapping her hands together aggressively. "Thanks for the great tips, kiddo—I'm gonna take it from here, okay?" She sidled up to Jack and gave his shoulder a squeeze. I watched in wonder as all of the boys moved through Belinda's choreography with increasing ease. Jenny leaned in close to my ear.

"So—what are *you* gonna do to impress her now?" she asked quietly.

I was thrown by the question.

"What do you mean?" I asked. "Like in my audition tomorrow?"

"Well, I just mean . . ." Jenny hesitated, then

pointed to Jack as all the soccer boys followed his every move.

"He's pretty much gonna be Belinda's favorite now, you know?"

I suddenly felt very uncomfortable.

"Not necessarily," I said, shifting in my seat.

"I'm not trying to say, like, you should be jealous or anything," Jenny rushed to clarify. "It's just that I know you want Belinda to like you, so . . ."

"So?"

"So—" Jenny took in a deep breath, then once again nodded toward the stage, where Jack had just made the seemingly impossible possible.

"So it's just gonna be hard to beat *that.*"

-JACK-

"As its name implies, music from this time went through a period of invention, a period of renewal."

We were nearing the end of music class the following day, and Mr. Hennessy was struggling to hold our attention with a lesson on music of the Renaissance. Though he spoke of lutes and mambas with enthusiasm (which for him meant peeking his spectacles over the piano and speaking in a voice barely louder than a whisper), there was clearly something else on the minds of his students. Looking around, I saw that the eyes of my classmates were completely glazed over. Our shared daydream was not one of minstrels and

monarchs but of the audition happening in just
a few hours. Although we'd survived Belinda's
nearly impossible dance call, today we'd be
singing and reading scenes.

No, I can't, I read off my audition sides, which
Lou had highlighted in purple. ("My audition
dress is purple," she'd said. Leave it Lou to plan
her audition outfit days in advance.)

Why not? Adelaide would respond.

Because, well, I mouthed, *I have to go to a prayer
meeting.*

Lou had been right—the scene Belinda had
chosen to use was the one before the song "Sue
Me," where Nathan tells Adelaide, truthfully, that
he has to go to a prayer meeting—but because
he lies to her so frequently she thinks the prayer
meeting is his biggest lie yet. Adelaide accuses
him of breaking all the promises he's kept while
he keeps insisting how much he loves her. To
be honest, I was still pretty shaky on the lines.
Before yesterday, I'd had the false confidence
that I could read a take-out menu and still land a
leading role, but now with the arrival of twenty
new boys, I knew I needed to bring my A-game.

"At first instruments were thought to be

secondary, used only to accompany dances and choral singing."

As Mr. Hennessy droned on, my gaze drifted over to Lou sitting next to me. Of everyone in the class, she seemed to be in the deepest of dream states, staring straight ahead, raising her eyebrows and cycling through a series of smirks, apparently solidifying her acting beats, as well.

"Which is why it's called a *bladder pipe*," Mr. Hennessy warbled, causing me to snap back to attention. "Because the wind reservoir containing the reed was actually made out of an animal's bladder."

I looked around the room. Silence. Even a teacher speaking of digestive tracts couldn't break the pre-audition trance of our class. Like a well-timed stage manager cue, the door to the music room swung open, and in popped a haystack of red hair.

"Hey, Frank," Belinda said as she made her entrance. Suddenly the class perked up. It was astonishing how quickly the energy of a room changed when Belinda Grier walked into it.

"Mind if I take the last few minutes to chat with the kids about the auditions today?"

"Well, I was just—" Mr. Hennessy mumbled, gesturing to his worksheet.

"Thanks, darlin'," Belinda said, cutting him off and strutting to the center of the classroom. Mr. Hennessy shrugged, reaching for his weathered old briefcase.

"So, as many of you know, the acting and singing auditions for *Guys and Dolls* will take place at three thirty in the auditorium," she said as she sat down on the edge of the desk. She flicked one leg up and crossed it over her knee. "Everyone will get a chance to sing thirty-two bars of the audition cut that I posted online, but first, I'll be breaking you up into pairs to read with each other."

I looked over at Lou, and we shared a smile. Even with the soccer boys, it seemed pretty inevitable that Belinda would pair us together. After all, she had referred to us as her minions.

"First we'll be reading the Skys and Sarahs, followed by the Nathans and Adelaides, and lastly the Hot Box Girls and other gangsters."

Oh good, I thought. At least I'd have a round of auditions to skim through the sides one more time.

"If you haven't already, please contact your parents after school to let them know that auditions will be running *late*," she said, drawing out the *l* in *late* for dramatic effect.

"We have far more people auditioning than expected, and I want to give everyone a chance to prove themselves. Please come vocally warmed up and prepared to jump right in," Belinda said, hopping off the table. "I'll see you guys at three thirty. Oh, and Jack," she said, looking over at me. "Would you mind hanging back for a second? I want to speak with you about something."

My pulse quickened.

"Uh, sure thing." I nodded confidently.

The bell let out its lunchtime cry and everyone jolted to their feet, cramming their worksheets into their backpacks.

What could Belinda want to talk to me about? I wondered. Between impromptu performances, jaw-dropping anecdotes, and the seeming ability to make an entire soccer team materialize, I'd learned to expect the unexpected from this woman. I looked over at Lou, who packed up her bag slowly.

"She doesn't want to talk to me, too?" she muttered.

"I don't know," I replied. "What do you think it's about?"

Lou gave me a shrug and walked to the door.

"See you in the lunchroom," she called back, disappearing into the stream of hungry middle-schoolers. I looked over at Belinda, who was already looking at me with a syrupy smile.

"Thanks for staying to have a chitchat," she said, walking around the table and grabbing a chair. "Here, take a seat. Okay if you hang here for a minute? You only have lunch, right?"

"Yeah," I said, lowering myself into the chair.

"Great!" she exclaimed, sitting down in the chair across from me. "Since day one I've wanted a chance to talk shop with you. You know, pro to pro. I remember thinking on that first day, *What a crazy coincidence, getting to share a classroom with another Broadway baby.*"

"Totally." I smiled politely.

"I was so tickled watching you take charge yesterday and help those jocks with my dance steps. Even *I* began to worry that they might never figure it out, but you just swooped right on in there and set them straight," she said, snapping her fingers. "I could tell I was watching someone who was used to thinking on his feet, and I have to say, it was pretty fun to see."

I had a feeling this was what Belinda wanted to talk about. Admittedly, I'd been on a bit of a high since successfully convincing the boys to stay and finish the dance call.

"So I just wanted to have a chance to tell you that in person," Belinda said. "You know? Face-to-face."

"Sure thing." I nodded. "Hey, I was happy to help."

Belinda sat there for a second just looking at me, which made me begin to feel a little tense.

"So, Jack," she said, breaking the silence. "Have you ever heard of a show called *Top Heavy*?"

"Um, I don't think so," I replied. It wasn't often that a musical was mentioned that I hadn't at least *heard* of.

"I'm not surprised. Neither has anyone," Belinda said dryly. "But would you mind if I told you a little story?" she asked, folding her hands on the desk.

"Sure." I nodded.

"Well," she began, "*Top Heavy* was the show in 1994 that everyone wanted to be a part of. It was a new musical directed by Gladys Franklin with a cast of *thirty* dancers, can you believe it?"

"Wow, that hardly ever happens on Broadway," I replied. "Not since—"

"*A Chorus Line.* Exactly," she said, cutting me off. "So you can imagine everyone in New York was breaking their backs to get an appointment. *Literally.*"

As she spoke, she began tapping her fingernails against the desk like a metronome.

"After three months of callbacks, they finally chose their cast and shipped everyone up to Boston for the out-of-town tryout. Each dancer was at the top of their game, and the producers began throwing money at it like high rollers at a casino. Everyone kept saying it was a dream job. And perhaps it was"—she leaned back in her chair—"until rehearsals began."

I felt a chill rush up my back. Like many actors, I had a guilty fascination with Broadway flops. I leaned in closer.

"Now Gladys Franklin was one of those *downtown* directors. She encouraged everyone to find their own style, and when it came time to stage numbers, she tried to showcase every dancer's specialties, even allowing some of them to choreograph entire phrases. A dream job indeed, right?"

At this point Belinda reached into her purse and pulled out a shiny black tube of lipstick. "Week three, she began to assemble the show." Belinda began dabbing lipstick on her bottom lip between sentences. "Gladys began to realize that because everybody had contributed choreography, the whole thing looked disjointed. When she tried to make cuts, people began freaking out. *Why was my number scrapped while hers was four minutes long?* Dancers started sabotaging one another's numbers. The dressing rooms turned into war zones, and by opening night all they had to show for themselves was a big, old, hot mess," Belinda said, smacking her lips together. "The *Globe* came and reviewed it, called it out for the disaster it was, and we closed by the end of the week, scrapping the entire Broadway run."

"*We?*" I said, sitting up in my chair. "You were in that cast?"

"Oh yeah," Belinda said, raising an eyebrow. "I was one of the leads. I was told I would finally be catapulted out of the chorus and into the spotlight, where I belonged, maybe even land a Tony nomination."

"Whoa," I whispered under my breath, genuinely stunned.

"So the reason I'm telling you this, Jack," Belinda said, replacing the cap of her lipstick, "is I've seen firsthand what happens when you don't have a clear leader—someone that everyone respects and looks to for guidance."

Belinda leaned forward in her chair, bringing her face close to mine.

"It becomes catastrophic."

I felt the hairs on the back of my neck stand up.

"Now, I know you may have seen some good cast and creative team collaborations in your time on Broadway, but it's different here. Not everyone's a professional like you and me. People *need* leadership," she emphasized with her scratchy voice.

"Which got me thinking," she said, wagging a finger in my direction. "We're not so different, you and me. Now, I remember just this summer reading an article on Broadway World about a little switcheroo that went down in a new show . . . *The Big Apple*, was it?"

I gulped, feeling my face getting hot.

"Um, yes," I murmured.

"I'm not going to pretend to know what went down there. That's your business and no one else's—"

"My voice changed," I interrupted. If I'd learned one thing from winter vacation, it was that it's better to give voice to your fears than to let them fester. "My voice changed, and I couldn't sing the show, so I got replaced," I said clearly. "That's one of the reasons my parents moved here."

Belinda gave me a look. It was the same look I'd seen the morning she'd arrived, when I told her my last name.

"Oh, honey, I'm sorry." She frowned. "That must have been hard for you."

I shrugged.

"Well, we're in a unique position here," she said softly. "You and me. We both know what it's like . . . having our dreams plucked from us."

Belinda reached across the desk and gave my arm a little squeeze.

"Now, you're auditioning for the role of Nathan Detroit this afternoon, right?" she asked, leaning back in her chair.

"Um, yes," I said, my mouth suddenly dry.

"Of course." Belinda chuckled. "And I know you

would be brilliant. I just worry that you're getting a little"—she squinted slightly, raising her pointer finger in the air—"distracted. Now that all these soccer boys have shown up, there's a much bigger talent pool, and I bet a lot of them would be great Nathans, too. Especially after what happened with *The Big Apple*, I'd just hate for you to use all that energy helping your competition instead of focusing on getting the role we both know you deserve."

I tried to scrunch the muscles in my face into a smile.

"So I want you to do me a favor, kiddo," Belinda said sweetly. "Today at auditions, I want you to knock it out of the park. Focus on your Nathan Detroit material, and let's prove to everyone what it means to be a Broadway professional. Forget about what those people in New York told you you could or couldn't do. Just do the best you can." She winked at me. "And this time, why don't you try leaving the directing to me?" She raised her voice when she said this, her words slightly echoing.

I sat in my chair, frozen, my sneakers glued to the linoleum floor. I didn't know how to feel. On one hand, it felt good to have someone who knew what it was like losing a job on Broadway, but on the other, I couldn't ignore the surge of guilt rushing through my body. Thinking back to the dance call yesterday, my only intention was to be helpful. I hadn't realized that reaching out to my classmates could lead to *catastrophe*.

"You know, I'm so glad we had this talk, Jack," she said, standing up and pushing in her desk chair. She walked around to where I was seated and stared down at me. "Why do you look so nervous, hon?" she asked. "I'm not upset or anything. I just wanted to make sure we're both on the same page. So are we?"

Even though she hadn't said anything mean, I felt like I was in trouble. Even though a smile spread across her face, something in her eyes made me feel a little uneasy.

"Yes." I nodded quickly, standing up. "Yes, ma'am."

"Aw," she said, opening her arms wide, bracing for a hug. "Well, thanks so much for the chitchat."

Her arms wrapped around me, pulling me in tight. I prayed she couldn't feel how fast my heart was beating.

Eleven

-LOUISA-

Jenny and I were practically finished with our lunch when Jack finally appeared in the cafeteria, scanning the room for our table. He spotted me waving and headed over.

"Sorry, guys," he said, taking a seat across from us.

"Don't be sorry," said Jenny, "you're the one who has to wolf down his lunch in eight minutes."

"What did Belinda want?" I asked, trying to sound nonchalant. I wanted so badly for it not to bug me that Belinda asked to talk to Jack and not me, but unfortunately it did. When we first met her, Belinda made it seem like the two of us were her go-to kids. But after Jack's heroic turn as Dance Wizard the day before, it seemed pretty obvious that she only needed him.

"Oh, uh . . . she wanted to talk shop," Jack replied. My stomach twinged. I began to silently lecture myself, explaining that it was only natural that Belinda would want to share her professional experiences with someone who truly understood them. And hadn't I been the one to tell Belinda about Jack's professional accomplishments? How could I feel both proud and jealous of my friend at the same time?

"So, like . . . did you guys swap a bunch of Broadway stories?" I asked as casually as I could.

"Uh, yeah, kind of," Jack said vaguely, reaching into his lunch bag for one of his mom's whole wheat veggie wraps. *Of course they did*, I thought, imagining them laughing about their theatrical escapades and all the fun people they had in common.

"Did she thank you for saving the day yesterday?" asked Jenny.

Rather than answer, Jack took a big bite of his wrap and began chewing vigorously.

"Oh, right," said Jenny, peering at the clock

above the vending machines. "You better eat fast."
She got up from the table.

"I'll see you guys at three thirty. *Please come
vocally warmed up and prepared to jump right in . . .*"
Jenny grinned and strutted off, pleased with her
Belinda impression. I felt a jolt of nerves race
through my arms and legs as I thought about the
auditions, wishing I had more time to prepare,
more time to come up with something that would
really knock Belinda's socks off this afternoon.
I watched Jack chewing furiously. Even though
I knew he was rushed, I needed to ensure that my
Adelaide was just right, so I asked, "Would you
mind if we read through our sides together one
more time? Really quick?"

Jack wiped the corner of his mouth with the
back of his hand and stuffed the remainder of his
veggie wrap into his lunch bag.

"Yeah, totally—I was actually gonna ask you
the same thing."

"Oh," I said with relief, "awesome!"

I reached for the sides sticking out of my
backpack, and as I sat back up I noticed that Jack
was biting the inside of his lip, a telltale sign he
was nervous. *What does he have to worry about?*

I thought. *He's the last person who should have audition jitters.*

At three thirty our auditorium looked like "Pandemonium" from *The 25th Annual Putnam County Spelling Bee*. While there wasn't a revolt underway like in the *Spelling Bee* song, there were still kids *everywhere*—in the aisles, on the stage, crowded around the piano. Also it was really *loud*. The sounds of kids working on their sides, singing through their thirty-two bars, plus twenty soccer players horsing around because they didn't know what else to do . . . It was chaotic. Once again I thought of poor Mrs. Wagner, and how she never would have managed to draw this kind of crowd— certainly not with any soccer boys. Belinda had worked some serious magic.

No sooner had that thought crossed my mind when the magician herself appeared from the wings, holding her clipboard and carrying a bullhorn.

"Good afternoon, all you Guys and Dolls!" she greeted us through the bullhorn. **"I practically shouted myself hoarse yesterday, so I'm using**

this today—I always love a prop! So listen up:
We will begin in just a couple minutes, so please
get yourselves organized by taking a seat in the
designated character areas—you will find that I
have sectioned off the seats into different roles:
Sarahs over there, Skys next to the Sarahs, and
so on and so forth. You do not need to be a rocket
scientist to figure out my system . . ."

Her last few words fell away as she lowered the
bullhorn mid-sentence to adjust her leg warmers.
I located the section designated "Adelaide," then
spotted Jack in the "Nathan" section across the aisle
and made my way toward him. Jack's shoulders
were hunched as he stared down at his hands,
murmuring to himself what I could only guess
were lines from the show.

I sidled up to him, hoping he'd compliment
my outfit. Jenny had helped me put together quite
an ensemble in preparation for today's audition.
Accessorizing my purple dress (A-line, cotton,
boring) in ways I never could have, she added a
belt ("to create more of a waist"), and a red silk
scarf that she tied in a bow around my neck ("to
make you look more old-timey"). The best and final
touch was a vintage purse that had belonged to

her great-grandmother, dating back to the 1930s.
A deep purple clutch purse made with silk and
embroidered with shiny black beads, it seemed
the perfect item for a gangster's showgirl/fiancée.
When I'd asked Jenny if she wanted to use it for the
audition, she'd given me a look.

"Please," she'd said with a wry smile. "You don't
have to be polite. I'm just there to dance. *You* need
to pull out all the stops."

Jack was concentrating so intensely that he
didn't even notice I was standing next to him.

"Ahem." I cleared my throat. Jack looked up.

"Oh, hey," he said. "Awesome purse." While he
didn't say anything else about my outfit, I was
pleased that he at least appreciated the coolest part
of it.

"I like that vest," I offered, taking in the fact
that he, too, had made an effort to look the part.

"Thanks," he replied softly.

"Think we're ready?" I asked. "Anything we
should go over?"

Before he had a chance to respond, Belinda's
bullhorn was put to use once again.

"All right, everybody!" she trumpeted. **"We're going to start with Skys and Sarahs!"**

For the next forty-five minutes, Jack and I sat anxiously across the aisle from each other, watching our classmates pair off to read the scene where expert gambler Sky Masterson introduces himself to Sister Sarah Brown after having accepted a bet from Nathan that he could convince her to go to Havana, Cuba, with him. Sarah, a pure and straightlaced woman who works at a local church mission, naturally resists his advances at first. The scene culminates in a big smooch—but of course Belinda wasn't going to make any of the kids do that in the audition. Nevertheless, that didn't stop Tanner from teasing poor Bridget Livak that he was going to kiss her anyway.

"I'm a serious actor now," he said mockingly as they arrived onstage. "I just want everything to be real." Bridget turned beet red and played the whole scene like she was being pursued by a serial killer. In a weird way, it worked. Bridget was really good.

Finally, at around four thirty, Belinda announced that we'd be moving on to the Nathans and Adelaides. As Jack and I exchanged nervous glances, I noticed the hair around his ears and at the base of his neck was damp with sweat. It made me think of the last time we were at an audition together, when he arrived sweaty and out of breath at the *Into the Woods* auditions—but that was because he'd come straight from abandoning the school's soccer tryouts. Odd that soccer played a part in these auditions, too. **"All right, let's start with Lou Benning and Broadway's very own Jack Goodrich!"** Belinda bellowed through the bullhorn. She looked over at Jack and flashed a grin.

"Let's show 'em how it's done on the Great White Way!" Blushing, Jack stood up and straightened his vest. I tried not to let Belinda's "Great White Way" comment throw me; if anything, I hoped it would motivate me even more to impress her. As we walked down the aisle toward the stage together Jack whispered, "Break a leg."

"You too," I whispered back.

Once onstage, I felt my mouth go dry. Even though I'd rehearsed it over and over again, the scene we were about to read now looked unfamiliar in my hands. The height of the stage, the sea of faces staring at us, and the sound of my heart pounding in my ears made me feel unsteady. But then I looked at Jack, whose face, while tense, was

still reassuring. Each taking a deep breath, we
began our scene.

"Adelaide!"

"Oh! What a coincidence!"

*"Adelaide, did Nicely explain to you about tonight?
I hope you ain't sore about it?"*

*"Oh please! Let us not have a vulgar scene. After
all, we are civilized people—we do not have to conduct
ourselves like a slob."*

Our classmates' reactions went from suppressed
giggling to full-out laughter, within only the
first few lines of dialogue. There is nothing more
confidence-boosting than laughter when you're
doing comedy—it's like oxygen to a fire. And both
Jack and I were burning up the stage.

"Nathan, why can't we elope right now?"

"Because—well, I got to go to a prayer meeting."

"Nathan. This is the biggest lie you ever told me!"

At the end of my last line, our classmates
erupted in applause, making me both slightly
embarrassed and elated. Jack and I walked off the
stage and back to our seats, where the kids sitting
near us high-fived us as we passed.

"You guys were awesome!"

"That was so funny!"

"You're so good together!"

I couldn't have felt better. Before sitting down, I grabbed Jack's elbow. "Great job," I said.

"You too," he said, collapsing into his seat. He looked exhausted.

From the front row of the audience came an announcement:

"Hey, guys, let's take a quick five, okay? I forgot to give you a break. Go grab some water, run to the bathroom. But seriously—no more than five minutes!"

Instantly, there was a mass exodus of kids herding through the double doors of the auditorium. I started to follow, thinking a drink of water would actually be pretty nice, when Belinda's amplified voice stopped me:

"Louisa Benning, would you meet me by the piano for a moment?"

My voice sounded mouse-like in response: "Okay."

I turned to Jack, eyebrows raised. He gave a tiny shrug and bit the inside of his lip.

Belinda, now standing, gestured for me to join her as she rested her elbows on the piano, her back to the auditorium. It was clear that she did not want other people to hear whatever she was about to say.

"So," she said as I joined her at the piano, "you've got quite a handle on this material." The way she said it made me unsure as to whether she was praising me or not.

"Well, we practiced a lot," I said, thinking not only was that the safest response but that I should give Jack equal credit.

"It showed; it definitely showed," she said, playing with one of her dangly earrings.

"Anyway," she continued, "we've got quite a lot of Guys to choose from now, don't we?"

"Yes, we do," I replied simply, not knowing if I was really supposed to be answering the question. Belinda merely nodded, and tapped her red nails on the shiny ebony surface of the piano.

"It's pretty great," I added, still wondering why exactly she'd called me over.

"It *is* great," Belinda continued, finally, "but now it's almost an embarrassment of riches—there's so *many* of them, I don't how I'm ever going to decide who to cast in what part."

I had butterflies in my stomach. Belinda was talking to me like I was her equal, and it was exciting. After wondering earlier whether she'd chosen Jack as her favorite, I was now suddenly optimistic that she hadn't forgotten me, after all.

Belinda placed a hand on my shoulder.

"If you don't mind, Lou, I'm going to have you read with a bunch of them. I'll have a better shot at casting them properly if there's someone on that stage who really knows what they're doing, you know? Someone who can bring out the talent in other people." I was instantly flattered. *Someone who can bring out the talent in other people* felt like one of the best compliments I'd ever received.

"S-sure," I stammered.

"Thanks, darlin'."

Belinda flashed her signature smile, squeezed my shoulder, and gave me a little push, indicating that I should return to my seat. Kids were filing back into the auditorium. I felt a rush of excitement as I made my way up the aisle. Even though I'd only danced and read one scene, even though I hadn't sung a note, it was looking like I had a pretty good shot at playing Adelaide! Inside I was doing cartwheels and jumping up and down, but on the outside I was simply walking toward my seat, squeezing my hands together in an effort to contain my elation.

"What were you talking to Belinda about?"

Jack was eagerly awaiting my return. Why did he still look nervous? His audition had gone just as well as mine.

"She's gonna have me read with a bunch of the boys," I said, "so they can read with a girl who's had some experience, I guess."

"Oh. That's cool," said Jack, though he sounded a little skeptical. As I looked at him I realized what exactly I was feeling: *satisfaction.* Yesterday Jack had been the hero, teaching the soccer boys how to dance. Today, in my way, I got to be the hero and teach the soccer boys how to *act.*

I knew I shouldn't feel like I was competing with my best friend. But Belinda's asking me to read with the other boys made me feel like I was just as talented as Jack. Maybe she'd ask *me* to stay behind after class one day; maybe she and *I* would get to swap stories.

Belinda's voice once again came blasting through her bullhorn.

"Okay, everybody! We're back! Let's continue with Louisa Benning reading Adelaide and Martin Howe reading Nathan!"

Both Jack and I looked up, startled.

"Nathan?" I blurted out, fortunately out of Belinda's earshot. When she'd asked me to read with the other boys, I had naturally assumed that they would be reading other roles. After all, there were so many to be cast: Nicely Nicely, Benny Southstreet, Harry the Horse, Big Jule, just to name a few. As far as I was concerned, Jack had just set the bar impossibly high for the role of Nathan Detroit. But who was I to question Belinda's audition methods? She was a pro. Jack was still looking concerned as I made sure my sides were in the proper order.

"Hey, no one will be as good a Nathan as you," I assured him. "Plus Belinda worships you. You seriously have nothing to worry about."

"Yeah," he said, forcing a smile. "I hope you're right."

There would be time later to convince Jack that his role was safe. Right now, I needed to prove to Belinda that everything she'd said about me was true. I took a deep breath and headed toward the stage.

Chapter

Twelve

-JACK-

The cast list was posted first thing Monday
morning. Belinda had told us at the end of our
auditions that it would be on the bulletin board
outside the music room as early as eight a.m.,
which meant that at 8:03 a.m., I found myself
hesitating in the stairwell and worrying about
what I might find once I arrived in the basement. I
wasn't worried about Lou. Belinda had practically
hung her name on the marquee, making her read
with more than a dozen Nathans. But with only one
time up at bat, would Belinda even remember me?

"Time to rip off the Band-Aid," Lou said as we
trudged down the stairs.

"Look at that!" Lou squealed as she pointed to the printed names on the yellow bulletin board. "I got Adelaide and, *phew*, you got Nathan," she said over the sound of excited castmates. "See, I told you. I knew we had nothing to worry about."

Lou gave me a big hug, and there it was. The stars had aligned after all. Jack and Louisa were back at it again, playing opposite each other in an exciting musical classic. Our production was sure to be the biggest ever to hit Shaker Heights Middle School. Everything was going perfectly. So why did I have a feeling it was all about to come tumbling down?

Lou clapped her hands together. "I'm going to go find Jenny and tell her our fantastic news."

I watched as her pink Converse shoes pranced up the stairs, leaving me alone in the basement.

"Congratulations," a woman's voice called from behind me.

I spun around to find Belinda standing against the wall, arms crossed.

"Glad to see you took our little conversation to heart," she said softly.

"Yeah . . . thanks," I muttered.

I knew I should have been excited, but

underneath Belinda's "congratulations" I sensed something threatening.

"Now, you know that I'm going to be expecting a lot from you," she said in a firm voice. "Some would argue that Nathan Detroit is the biggest role of the show, and given your pedigree, I'm really going to need you to lead by example."

"Of course." I nodded.

"I'm going to be a lot harder on you than the rest of the cast, but that's only because I know you can handle it. Think of yourself as . . ." Belinda hesitated. "The star quarterback. If I were your coach, I'd push you to your limits knowing what you're capable of. Do you follow?"

"Yes."

"Okay, darlin'. See you in rehearsal." She winked, nodding toward the cast list. "We've got a great team."

Belinda was right about one thing—she had assembled a pretty amazing group. Sebastian Maroney had surprised us all with a rich baritone voice in his audition for Sky Masterson, singing "Luck Be a Lady" like a teenage Frank Sinatra.

Bridget Livak, a shy, mousy eighth-grader, had gotten the role of Sarah Brown. I'd sort of dismissed her when she struggled quietly through the dance call, but when she opened her mouth the following day, a beautiful high soprano rang through the auditorium. Jenny was cast as a Hot Box Girl and the lead dancer in the Havana sequence (a scene in which Sarah, having agreed to accompany Sky down to Cuba, finally lets her hair down). In a true stroke of genius, the role of Big Jule, the meanest, scariest of all the gangsters, went to Tanner Falzone. I'd have no trouble pretending to be terrified of him during the crapshooter scene in Act 2. Best of all, Lou and I would get to spend the next two months playing the great comic duo. It seemed like we'd hit the jackpot.

The first day of rehearsal we circled around the piano, separated into vocal sections. Mr. Hennessy began teaching "Sit Down, You're Rockin' the Boat," the biggest production number in the show. I watched as boys flipped through their music, struggling to follow along as each section was taught a different line of harmony. As Mr. Hennessy plunked out the soprano line, Adam, an eighth-grade soccer player who'd been cast as Harry the Horse, leaned over to me.

"Where the heck am I supposed to be looking at?" he said, pointing to the many staffs of music notes on the page. "It's like it's Chinese!"

"Don't worry about sight-reading," I whispered back. "Just make a voice memo on your phone the next time Mr. Hennessy plays your part. That way you can go home and listen to it later."

"Jack," Belinda's voice shot across the theater, causing Mr. Hennessy to fumble his piano playing and the entire room to fall silent. Her voice softened. "Did you have a question, hon?"

I opened my mouth, ready to explain that I was just helping to clear something up, but suddenly remembered the conversation I'd had with her about authority just a few days ago.

"No, ma'am," I called back. "Sorry to disturb the rehearsal."

Belinda wasn't joking when she said she'd be hard on me. And to be honest, I was cool with it at first. She'd obviously been in the business a long time, and perhaps her feedback would help me down the line.

The next week we began staging. First up was the scene where Adelaide runs into Nathan the evening of their anniversary. Belinda had directed us to play the scene sitting on a rehearsal cube. *"Look, honey—about your present,"* I said, wringing my hands. *"I was going to get you a diamond wristwatch with a gold band and two rubies on the side."*

Lou gasped. *"Nathan, you shouldn't have."*

"It's all right," I replied, swinging my legs and facing away from her. *"I didn't."*

"Stop!" Belinda barked, waving her arms like a crossing guard. Lou and I peered out into the audience.

"Jack, sweetie, correct me if I'm wrong," Belinda said calmly, "but didn't I already explain? The cube is just a stand-in. The real park bench will have armrests on the sides, so you won't be able to move your legs like that."

"Oh, okay." I swallowed.

"I'm sure it was the same when you were on

Broadway, honey," Belinda said, chuckling to herself. "I can't imagine you rehearsed on the set the whole time."

I forced an uncomfortable laugh.

"I'm going to need you to really try to stay focused," Belinda said. "I can't keep stopping rehearsal to give you these technical notes."

"Sure thing," I said with a nod.

I looked over at Lou, who eyed me with slight concern, but I shrugged it off, signaling that I was fine.

"Okay, let's take it back to Adelaide's entrance," Belinda called out to the room. "Oh, and, Lou," she said, smiling broadly, "I love what you're doing with the voice. It's just adorable!"

Week two was under way, and even though I continued showing up prepared and ready to work, it felt like I had a giant "kick me" sign on my back. When I would try to land a joke: *You're playing for laughs. On Broadway, don't they want you to play the honesty?"* If I would enter from the wrong wing: *"Didn't they teach you on Broadway to write down your blocking as soon as it's given to you?"* Even if I tried to get an early start on memorizing: *"I'd rather you hold a script than be sloppily off-book. I don't think Abe Burrows would appreciate you fudging his dialogue."*

I knew that Belinda was going to treat me differently, that she'd be harder on me if I made mistakes, but I didn't realize I'd be the *only* one scolded for making them. When we got to the scene where all the gangsters entered with carnations, Tanner was nowhere to be found.

"I happen to be entertaining a very prominent guest tonight. I think you might have heard of him," Adam said in a thick, nasally voice. *"I would like you to meet Big Jule from Chicago."* He gestured over to a spot onstage where a tough-looking Tanner was supposed to be standing.

Instead, Tanner was goofing off in the wings, trying to make the Hot Box Girls laugh by stuffing a pillow under his soccer jersey. Lou, ever alert, pushed him onstage, the pillow still spilling out the bottom of his shirt.

"Well, look at you," Belinda guffawed.

"Haha, yeah sorry, I forgot I was in this scene,"

Tanner mumbled, red-faced.

"Oh, don't worry, honey." Belinda giggled. "We
still have more than a month left to rehearse."

Even though my scolding sessions with Belinda
were becoming more and more frequent, I was at
least able to find comfort in the fact that the soccer
boys were being nice to me. And they were pretty
good in the show, too. While their singing left a
little to be desired, and their accents wandered
from New York to Alabama to Great Britain and
back again, their energy onstage was infectious.
They worked like a team, slapping each other's
backs and hamming it up. It was hard to imagine
that just a few short weeks ago these guys were
scary to me. One afternoon Coach Wilson popped
in as we rehearsed "The Oldest Established," a song
that involved me being lifted up and flipped over
the soccer boys' shoulders. As the song drew to a
close, I stepped forward to begin the dialogue back
into the scene.

*"Gentlemen, do not worry. Nathan Detroit's crap
game will float again."*

"Stop!" Belinda cried out from the front row.

The room went silent. "Jack, I can't hear a word you're saying!"

The boys turned and shielded their eyes from the lights, looking out into the audience.

"I know on Broadway you're used to having microphones and amplification, but here in Shaker Heights I'm going to need you to PRO-JECT!" she yelled.

"Sorry," I mumbled. "You got it."

"See? Even now," Belinda said, flinging her hands in the air. "I need you to SPEAK. UP."

My face got hot. I tried to hide my frustration. I wasn't an idiot. I understood the need to be heard, but wouldn't I seem like a crazy person if I just shouted every line at the top of my lungs?

"YES, MA'AM," I said in my most resonant stage voice.

"Thank you," she said, taking a seat in the squeaky auditorium chair. "Once again from the top . . . for Jack."

As we got back into place I looked at the guys, but they avoided my gaze, not wanting to be associated with the kid who'd messed up, again. I peered out into the audience, where Coach Wilson was leaning over to Belinda, whispering something in her ear. She looked directly at me and gave a dry laugh, swatting him away. Mr. Hennessy began plunking the intro as Coach Wilson got up to leave. Just before exiting, he turned and gave me a little salute, an apologetic look in his eyes.

Oh, but the worst thing? The thing that made the experience all the more frustrating? Even though I was miserable, Lou could not have been happier. Belinda doted on her like a proud stage mom, throwing compliments like roses and clapping extra hard after every one of her songs. We'd do scenes where Belinda would laugh after every Adelaide joke but sit there stone-faced through all my Nathan punch lines.

I'd show up early and ready to work but immediately get yelled at.

"You know, for a guy with multiple Broadway credits, you really ought to remember to bring a highlighter to rehearsal."

Meanwhile Lou would stroll in and be congratulated for something like, I don't know, *remembering to breathe oxygen.*

I began feeling that emotion I hated, that

toxic green blob that I could feel in my stomach.
It was something I'd felt a few times for people
back in New York but never toward my best friend:
jealousy.

"You hangin' in there?" Lou asked me after
rehearsal one day. "It seems like Belinda's pretty
tough on you."

"No, it's fine," I replied.

"Really?" Lou asked.

"Yes, really," I replied. "Just leave it, Lou."

Lou looked at me for a few more seconds, and
then shrugged her shoulders. "Okay, if you say so."

Of course it wasn't fine, but how could I expect
Lou to understand when she was having the time
of her life?

I'd been managing to keep it all together until
exhaustion got the better of me toward the end
of our fourth week. I'd been up the night before
studying for a science test.

We began blocking the scene before Lou's big
number, "Adelaide's Lament." Lou and I set our
scripts down on the edge of the stage.

"*I couldn't be engaged for fourteen years, could*

I?" Lou squeaked in her perfected Adelaide voice. *"People don't do that in Rhode Island. They all get married."*

A raspy laugh heaved from the audience, obviously Belinda's.

I cocked my head and delivered my next line. *"Then how come it's such a tiny state?"*

Lou wasn't even able to get her next line out because the sound of Belinda's voice rang through the auditorium like a fire alarm.

"Stop!" The room went deadly quiet. "Jack, the line isn't *'Then how come it's such a tiny state?'"* Belinda said stiffly. "It's *'Then why is it such a small state?'"*

"Oh," I replied quietly, "yeah, sorry."

Belinda scowled at me, a fiery look shooting from her eyes.

"Louisa, hon, would you mind taking five?" Belinda said with a big fake smile.

"Um, sure," Lou said, looking over at me hesitantly as she walked to the wings.

"Jack, can I speak with you downstage?" Belinda said firmly.

What now? I wondered as I trudged forward. Belinda took a deep breath.

"What's going on with you, Jack? Your focus is really off, and I worry we're not on the same page. I'm doing this for you," she said with earnest. "So I can get the best work out of you. I can't be the only one invested."

But I didn't believe her anymore. I didn't know why she was treating me this way, but I knew that we were definitely not on the same page.

"I'm sorry," I said, staring down at my dress shoes. "I'll do it better the next time."

"You know, it's always the *next time* with you," Belinda said, narrowing her eyes. "The *next time* you'll say it right. The *next time* you'll pick up your cues. I'm not sure what kind of directors you've worked with on Broadway, but the *next time* doesn't get you very far; it gets you fired."

A list of angry questions began to form in my head. Why was Sebastian allowed to call "line" every three minutes, but I'd get a tongue-lashing for rephrasing one tiny bit of dialogue? Why could Bridget perform an entire scene facing upstage, yet if I did it once, I'd be told off? Most of all: Why did Lou have to tell Belinda about my Broadway past? I cringed every time Belinda brought it up, knowing it would probably be used to emphasize a stupid mistake I'd made. Why couldn't I have just been another theater-loving local? But I didn't say any of these things. I just let her words gush over me like hot tar.

"All right, take five, kiddo," Belinda said, glancing at her wrist. "I'd suggest you spend that time rereading your script."

I didn't even wait for her to finish speaking before charging offstage and into the wings.

"Jack," I heard Lou call from behind me.

"What?!" I said loudly, not even bothering to turn and look at her.

"Whoa," she replied. "You okay? You seem kind of upset."

"Oh really?!" I shot back, whipping around to face her. "I'm glad you're noticing all the things wrong with me, too."

"What are you talking about?" Lou said, taking a step back. "I was just seeing if you were okay. You don't need to yell at me."

"Do I look okay?" I shrieked. "Ever since the stupid auditions, this show has been nothing but torture."

Lou looked completely surprised.

"It doesn't matter what I do, it's never good enough," I said, crossing my arms tight. "And not only that, but Belinda seems to feel the need to let everyone in our cast know about it."

Lou crossed her arms defensively. She opened her mouth to say something, but I cut her off.

"I hope you realize this is all your fault."

Chapter

Thirteen

-LOUISA-

"All *my* fault?"

I stared at Jack in disbelief. I was so mad. Was he serious? "What do you mean, all *my* fault?!"

Jack took a step toward me, angrily spitting out his words.

"That first day we met Belinda, you had to be all *'Jack was in this Broadway show, and that Broadway show . . . Jack's so amazing, Jack, Jack Jack . . .'* You made me her target. And all she's cared about ever since is putting me in my place."

Jack was angrier than I'd ever seen him. Even more startling was that he was directing that anger at me.

"I wasn't trying to make you her 'target,'" I sputtered. "I just wanted her to know that you'd been on Broadway, too!"

"Well, thanks a lot. She's done everything she can to use that against me."

"Huh?"

"Don't tell me you haven't noticed how differently she acts toward me than she does toward everyone else," Jack said, his face reddening. "I know you have."

The way he glared at me made me feel sick to my stomach. I did not want to be fighting with my friend, certainly not in the middle of rehearsing a show where we were playing opposite each other.

"Well, sure, I've noticed, sort of," I conceded, "but every time I've asked you if you're okay, you've said yes—"

"And every time I've said yes, you've looked relieved, so you can go back to being Belinda's 'perfect Adelaide' while I can go back to being her punching bag."

"You are not her punching bag!" I protested, though I suspected that nothing I said at this point was going to help.

"You're right, I'm her 'star quarterback.'" Jack rolled his eyes in disgust.

"What?"

The sick feeling in my stomach was suddenly replaced by a tightening in my chest.

"Nothing—it's not even true," Jack said. I could tell he was holding something back.

"No," I pressed him, "what are you talking about?"

He wouldn't look at me. "I don't believe her, but she told me she was going to hold me to a higher standard," he muttered. "She says that's why she's being so hard on me."

Now *I* started to feel angry.

"Because you're *so* much better than the rest of us?"

"That's not what I'm saying!"

"So then why *is* she treating you differently?"

"I don't know, I didn't ask her to—*you* did!"

Through clenched teeth I fought back, "Some of us might love it if Belinda held us to a 'higher standard.'"

"Oh gimme a break!" Jack said, his frustration mounting. "Belinda is obsessed with everything you do! Trust me, you don't want her 'special' treatment. All I feel is like the harder I work, the meaner she gets. So I'm working really hard for nothing. It's just . . . not worth it anymore."

His words hung in the air while I registered what he'd just said.

"Are you going to quit?" I asked, dreading his answer.

"Maybe."

Without thinking, I shot back, "You like to threaten that a lot, don't you?"

As soon as I said it I knew I'd gone too far. I might as well have slapped him in the face.

"Break's over! We're back!" Belinda called from the audience.

Jack looked past me toward the stage, his eyes filling.

"This is completely different from *Into the Woods*, and you know it," he said quietly, then marched past me, leaving me alone in the wings.

Thankfully, Belinda wanted to move on to the first Sky/Sarah scene after the break, so she dismissed the rest of the cast for the day. As Sebastian and Bridget shyly took their places

onstage to rehearse their love duet, "I'll Know,"
Jack bolted out of the auditorium as fast as he
could. Clearly he wanted to avoid any more contact
with me—or with anyone, for that matter. To be
honest, I wasn't ready to have any more contact
with him—I felt so ashamed of what I'd said.

Even though it was cold out, the air was dry
and crisp and I decided to walk home. I needed
some time alone to think.

Had Belinda really been that awful to Jack? I asked
myself as I marched through the cold, the tips of
my fingers growing numb under my backpack
straps. I felt ashamed all over again as I revisited
every compliment, every cheer of encouragement
that Belinda had given me over the past few weeks,
and realized that I had not once heard her extend
the same praise to Jack. I had obviously been too
busy enjoying her attention and trying to be the
perfect Adelaide to notice that the only feedback
Jack received from Belinda was critical. Even
though I was initially stung by the idea of Belinda
holding Jack to a higher standard than me, I started
to wonder whether Jack was right when he said
that he didn't believe her. But if she was lying, then
what was the *real* reason behind her behavior?

Aside from his professional background, I couldn't think of one thing that would have compelled Belinda to be so tough on him. Jack had worked really hard on his material; he was always prepared and ready to work. Everyone in the cast liked him; he'd been so helpful to them, particularly during the dance call . . .

The dance call.

With Jack's words ringing in my ears, I now suddenly remembered it in a different way. Belinda's face. The smile that looked so fake. The way she clapped harder than anyone else when the soccer boys were able to do the combination after Jack had broken down the moves for them. Like she was covering for something. And then there was our secret conversation by the piano, when Belinda told me she wanted me to audition with the other boys. If she had, in fact, been trying to put Jack in his place, then making him watch his best friend audition with his competition would have definitely sent a strong message. The more I thought about it, the more things came into focus. Suddenly a new picture of Belinda began to form in my head. A former theater star of Shaker Heights, a woman used to being seen as special for her talent

and her Broadway resume, was suddenly forced
to share the spotlight. And her sassy comments
about Jack's experiences on Broadway, the way she'd
singled him out, the way she'd embarrassed him in
front of the cast . . . everything started to make a
lot more sense. As I turned onto my street, I walked
briskly past my house toward a more important
destination.

"Belinda's jealous of you."
I stood on Jack's front porch, shivering like crazy
but determined to fix things between us.
"What?"
"Can I come in?"
Jack motioned for me to come inside, then
crossed his arms, waiting for me to say more.
"I walked all the way here from school, and I
thought about what you said, and you're right—
Belinda's been totally unfair. But it's because she's
jealous of you."
It all seemed so obvious now, and so ugly. I'd just
been too busy vying for Belinda's approval to notice.
I'd really wanted her to like me, because I'd really
liked her.

Jack opened his mouth to speak, but I wasn't finished.

"And I'm sorry that I was the one who started it all. I'm also *really* sorry for the other stuff I said. I didn't mean it."

"I'm sorry, too," Jack said, uncrossing his arms, "for blaming you. You said it yourself—Belinda would have found out that I've been on Broadway eventually." He paused. "And it's not your fault that she's been nice to you. I mean, she should be nice to you."

"Yeah, well, she should be nice to you, too," I said.

"You really think she's jealous of me?"

"I do."

"That's so weird."

"I know."

"Huh." Jack scratched the back of his neck.

"What?"

"Well, I wasn't going to talk about it, but . . ."

Jack proceeded to tell me about his private talk with Belinda, in which she'd basically told him to keep his mouth shut and let her be in charge. His story made me furious.

"You should have told me," I said once he was

finished. "She was obviously trying to scare you."

"Well, it worked," Jack admitted. "She made me feel like I'd done something wrong, and I was too embarrassed to talk about it. I thought if I could just get the part of Nathan and work really hard, she'd leave me alone."

"But she didn't," I said, wanting desperately to give Jack a much-needed hug.

"Yeah, whatever," he said, then looked at me in earnest.

"I don't want to ruin the show for you, Lou."

"You won't," I said adamantly, "but you might if you *quit* the show . . ."

Jack sighed.

"I'll give it some more time. Now that I know I can talk to you about it . . . I dunno, maybe it'll be easier to deal with her."

"You can talk to me whenever you want," I said, finally going in for the hug. We squeezed each other hard, then broke apart as Jack looked toward the kitchen. Whatever Mrs. Goodrich was making smelled delicious. "Hey—do you want to stay for dinner?" he asked. "Mom's making mulligatawny stew—it's really good. There's a lot of curry in it."

"Yeah, let me call my parents," I said, hugely relieved that we weren't fighting anymore. "I'd love to stay."

I spent the next day at school feeling nervous. Now that I had figured out the reason behind the Belinda/Jack conflict, would I be able to focus in rehearsal? Was there anything I could do to protect him? Maybe make some mistakes myself so she'd come after me instead of him? I just didn't know how I was going to react if and when Belinda decided to attack.

At three o'clock, as Jack and I approached the doors to the auditorium, I was feeling super tense. Jack must have sensed it, because he turned to me and said, "Relax, Lou. Belinda's not going to hack me to pieces with an ax or anything. She's just going to make me feel like an idiot."

"Yeah, okay," I said, nodding aggressively. Jack eyed me warily.

"Honestly, Lou, chill out," he said, opening the door for me. "This is my problem, not yours. Just ignore her if she comes after me. Promise?"

I kept nodding and forced myself to take a deep

breath as I entered the auditorium.

"It's 3:01, people!" shouted Belinda, pacing back and forth across the stage like a bedazzled panther. She wore black jeggings and a baggy black sweatshirt with a sequined top hat and cane embroidered on the front.

"We've been rehearsing for a month, and we still haven't run all of Act One, so let's get a move on! Everyone who's in Act One, Scene Six—get up here now to review!"

I took a swig from my water bottle and hurried toward the stage, going over my lines in my head.

I thought Scene 6 was pretty funny—it's when Nathan Detroit has rounded up all of the gangsters for his crap game but has to explain to a snooping Detective Brannigan what they're all doing together, and why they're all wearing carnations. One of the gangsters spies Adelaide approaching and comes up with a quick lie: They're there to throw Nathan a bachelor party. When she hears this, Adelaide squeals with delight. She thinks Nathan has decided to surprise her with a wedding. Waiting for the bus that morning, Jack and I had worked out a new bit that cracked us up. There's a line where Adelaide almost gives the gangsters away, saying to Nathan, "*But when I saw you standing here with all these fine gentlemen, I never dreamed it was a bachelor dinner. I thought it was a—*" and Nathan cuts her off by saying, "*Oh, it's a bachelor dinner. Yes, sir! A bachelor dinner.*" Jack suggested that he cut off my line by picking me up and squeezing me really tight so that I couldn't get the rest of my sentence out, which inspired me to make a sound like a mouse getting stepped on.

Once everyone was onstage, Belinda hopped down into the audience and sat in the front row, grabbing her clipboard off the floor.

"Let's take it from the top!" she shouted.

The boys spread themselves out across the stage as Grady Ayers, playing Benny Southstreet, began the scene: "*You all got your carnations?*"

I stood in the wings, waiting not only for my cue but for Belinda to say something snarky to Jack. Jenny and the rest of the Hot Box Girls were backstage, too, having designated stage right as their card-playing spot. As the scene went on, it seemed like Belinda was leaving Jack alone. She even snickered a couple times. By the time I heard my cue line, I was feeling more relaxed and cautiously optimistic that Jack would get through an entire scene without a Belinda intervention.

"*Good-bye, girls, see you tomorrow,*" I said as nasally as possible, entering backward and waving at the Hot Box Girls. (Jenny looked up from her card game to stick her tongue out at me.) The moment for the new bit arrived just a few lines later, and Jack's timing could not have been more perfect. My mouse squeak pierced the air, making all of the other boys crack up. Even Tanner guffawed. But the moment was short-lived.

"*QUIET.*"

Belinda's voice, stern and steely, put an abrupt end to the laughter. Jack set me down, and we both turned to look at her. *Please*, I thought, *whatever it is you're about to say—say it to me, too.*

"Jack—is that what I directed you to do?"

Maybe because he and I had talked, or maybe because he was just exhausted, Jack didn't look at the floor. He didn't bite the inside of his lip or do any of the things he normally did when he was uncomfortable or embarrassed. He just looked straight at Belinda, waiting for the critique.

"No," he said simply.

"Then . . . *why* did you do it?" she asked, trying to stare him down.

I blurted out, "Belinda, we both—"

"Lou, am I speaking to you?"

"No, but—"

"But nothing, then. Please stay out of this."

I looked at Jack, helpless, but he just kept looking at Belinda.

"Jack," Belinda continued, "I thought I made it clear that I was the director of this show, not you. Yet somehow you feel that rules don't apply to you."

My hands and feet started to tingle; everything was going numb and my ears started to hum. The other boys were shifting their feet from side to side as the air in the room grew thicker and hotter with awkwardness. I wondered if any of them knew that what was happening was wrong, or worse, if they thought it was amusing. I caught Jenny standing in the wings with the other Hot Box Girls, their card game abandoned as they watched Jack and Belinda with apprehension. But Jack didn't say a word, and Belinda seemed to become even more fueled by his silence.

"It's interesting," she went on, "I mean, if you're supposedly—what did Lou call you? Oh, right—'the Best of Broadway,' I can't even begin to imagine what the *worst* might be."

That was it. I felt something pop in my brain, like a firecracker. Even though Jack had assured me that Belinda was his problem, not mine, even though I had promised him that I'd ignore her, I couldn't keep the scream from exploding out of me: *"STOP IT!"*

Fourteen

-JACK-

Lou's voice blared through the auditorium like a tornado siren. Every muscle in my body seized up as a silence swept the room. My eyes darted to Belinda, then to Lou, then back to Belinda, who stood in the front row, speechless, her spider lashes blinking madly.

"Ex-*cuse* me?" she growled.

Lou's face looked as red as ketchup. Her hands began trembling at her sides.

"What did you just say?!" Belinda's voice grew louder.

I looked over at Lou, shaking my head with pleading eyes. This was never going to end well.

Even though Lou was one of the bravest people
I knew (she'd once brought Tanner to his knees
for making fun of me), this was different. Belinda
was a grown-up. Even more than that, she was a
teacher, and when you were a kid, talking back
to a teacher just wasn't something you did.

Lou swallowed hard and looked Belinda
straight in the eye.

"I said *stop it*," Lou replied quietly. "Stop yelling
at Jack like that."

Belinda's body recoiled in shock, like she'd been
slapped in the face.

Lou's breathing quickened as she took a step
downstage. "He's been working his butt off, and
all you do is pick on him," she said, confidence
growing. "Since the first day of auditions all he's
done is try to be helpful and make this show better.
You're supposed to be our leader," Lou shouted, her
voice straining. "But you're just being a bully!"

That was it. It was all over now. What was Lou
thinking? No excuses or apologies could get us out
of this one. Even though I willed myself to look at
Belinda, I couldn't do it. A wave of nausea rushed to
my stomach as I shifted my gaze to the wood grain
beneath my feet.

"Well, I'm *sorry*," Belinda's voice called. Her voice sounded scratchy, like someone waking up after a long night of sleep.

"I'm *so sorry* that I was trying to do my job." She punctuated her words dramatically. "See, Louisa, *honey*, I was under the impression that it was my job to make sure everyone said the right lines and did the right blocking." A strand of red hair had fallen from her bun, plunging down the center of her face like an angry scar. "So if you don't like the way I'm running this room"—she raised her voice—"I suggest you either *shut your mouth* or get out!"

A series of gasps emerged from the students behind us and from the girls crowded in the wings. I tried lifting my head, but it felt like a hundred pounds. I wanted to speak up and tell Belinda that Lou was just being overly protective, that we should get back to work and talk about this later, like next year or when we graduated from high school. But I did nothing. I just stood there.

"Humph," Belinda grunted, crossing her arms. "That's what I thought." She smiled smugly as she fixed Lou with her fiery stare.

My head began to throb. I closed my eyes

tightly, wishing for a way to undo the last minute and a half. After all, no scolding, no criticizing, no *bullying* could be worse than this. Just as I was about to open my eyes I heard the shuffling of shoes, a pair of Converses to be exact. They thumped down the stairs and past the front row of seats. I looked up to see Lou storming up the aisle like a soldier in combat. She snatched her coat off a chair and slammed her hands against the double doors, pushing through the exit without looking back.

"Well," Belinda said, straightening her sweatshirt. "Anyone *else* have a problem with how I'm directing this show?"

The cast stood frozen. No one made a sound.

"Sayonara," a girl's voice trumpeted from the wings. Out of the corner of my eye, I watched as Jenny brushed past the Hot Box Girls and onto the stage. She pranced down the stairs, breaking into an *across-the-floor* of ballet leaps and turns as she made her way up the aisle. Even though it was priceless, no one dared to laugh. She grabbed her dance bag and Lou's backpack from the seats and shoved her way through the heavy auditorium doors.

Belinda's face clouded over with anger. A thick vein pulsed in her forehead. She brushed back that same persistent strand of hair and crammed it behind her ear.

"Doesn't matter," she huffed. "If there's one thing we have too many of in this show, *it's girls.*"

A grunt sounded from the gangsters clumped around me. One of them marched across the stage, stomping down the stairs and joining Lou and Jenny in a dramatic exit. To my astonishment, it was Tanner Falzone.

"Well, here goes one of your guys," he called out as the doors slammed behind him.

Then something even crazier happened. Sebastian Maroney jogged to the stairs, turning to look back at his castmates before charging up the aisle. Then Adam Hull. Then Grady Ayers. Then Martin Howe. In less than a minute the entire soccer team had defected. Bridget Livak was the next of the girls, emerging from the wings, the black binder containing her script smacking the stage as she marched toward the exit. The rest of the cast followed suit, tossing their scripts on the floor before sweeping out of the auditorium. The only person left was me.

The final door slam ricocheted through my body. My feet felt like cinder blocks. I looked up slowly, finding myself face-to-face with my tormentor, the top hat and cane on her chest rising and falling as she took in one panicked breath after another. Her eyes darted frantically around the empty hall, searching for anything to land upon besides the last kid standing in front of her. But as the angry footsteps faded, it became clear that she'd have to face me alone, no audience to listen as she spewed another villainous rant.

"Well," she said after what felt like minutes of silence. "Bet that never happened to Mrs. Wagner."

She gave a dismissive laugh and looked around the room, as if expecting at any moment the cast would reappear and apologize for their hasty exit. I lifted my tongue to speak, but the words felt stuck in my throat.

"Oh, come on, Jack," she said. "I wasn't serious about you being *the worst of Broadway.* We both know Lou can be a little dramatic."

I just stood there, my feet refusing to move. My body felt numb, like I'd just been shot with one of those poison darts. Belinda crossed her arms as if to contain her agitation.

"Why are you still here?" she asked.

I searched my brain for a reason. I thought of my friends, huddled in the cold parking lot wondering if I would join them. I thought of the moment when Belinda first showed her ugliness to me, that day in the music room after the dance call when I'd dared to speak up. I thought of every insult she'd hurled at me, always making sure to highlight the fact that as a Broadway actor, I really should have known better.

"I don't know," I responded.

"Why don't you follow your classmates?" she said, pointing to the door. "There's obviously nothing left to do here. You got all your friends to leave, so why don't you just go? You don't have to rub it in."

"I'm not rubbing it in," I said, my throat becoming tight.

Whatever you do, I told myself, *do not let yourself cry in front of this woman.*

And then something strange happened. Belinda began shaking her head. She slumped into a seat. Her shoulders rose and fell as she sighed heavily.

"I know," she said after a moment. "I know you're not the kind of person who'd do that."

Her words startled me. I wasn't sure what to say. I wondered if maybe this was my chance. Whatever angry thoughts I was feeling, perhaps now was the time to say them. But she was right. I wasn't the kind of person who'd do that. I couldn't explain why, but I knew that whatever happened next wasn't going to be bad.

"It's because . . . you're strong," she continued. "Stronger than me."

She turned away, fixing her gaze on the pile of black binders left on the stage like old bonfire logs on a beach.

"Is that why you keep picking on me?" I asked.

This question seemed to knock the wind out of her. She raised her eyebrows and peered down at the floor.

"No," she muttered. "That's not why, Jack. That's not why."

From the hallway, I could hear the thrum of the janitor emptying a garbage can as a wordless tension hung in the air. Belinda gave a little laugh. "It's funny. Mike . . . I mean Coach Wilson," she corrected herself. "He asked why I was so hard on you. Thought I might be a little *out-of-bounds*. I gave him the same answer I kept giving you.

But he wondered if it might be because I felt . . ."
She trailed off. I watched her take in a deep breath,
her lips forming carefully like they were searching
for the right words.

"The truth is, Jack"—she shook out her hands—
"working with you . . . has been hard for me."

I scrunched my forehead in confusion. *Hard
for you?*

"Something I should have told you, when the
show I was in, *Top Heavy*, closed out of town, it was
really . . ." She hesitated. "Difficult. Everyone had
been telling me I was going to be a big deal, and
when that didn't happen, well . . ."

I stood there, silent. I knew I could just let her
struggle, watching her untangle the mess she'd
created, but deep down I knew exactly how she felt.

"I understand," I said, almost not recognizing
the sound of my own voice.

"What?" She looked up, surprised.

"People said the same things to me when I got
cast in *The Big Apple*. I know what that's like."

"But look at how you bounced back," she
replied.

"I don't know. When I saw *The Big Apple*, I was
really . . ." A warning flashed in my brain, *Maybe*

choose a different word than jealous. "It was really hard to watch."

She leaned in, clasping her hands between her knees. "To see something that was supposed to be yours?"

I nodded.

"Yeah. It's so tough. I spent twenty years trying to get back to a place where people thought I was a big deal, and when that didn't happen, I felt like a failure."

"When I saw *The Big Apple* I couldn't say anything to the kid who replaced me," I admitted. "I didn't even tell him *congratulations.*"

"I bet you were still a lot nicer to him than I was to you," Belinda said, raising an eyebrow.

"Well, I didn't tell him that *he was the worst of Broadway.*"

Belinda winced at the memory of her own words.

"Of course you didn't. I'm sure that boy looks up to you, just like how everyone looks up to you. I mean the way you got those soccer boys to dance."

"I thought you said that was bad."

She laughed to herself. "I said that because I wanted all the attention. It's silly, I know," she said, shaking her head. "But I thought coming home, I'd at least have that much. So when the first person I met had not only been on Broadway but had done more in a few years than I did in twenty . . ." She smiled. "Grown-ups don't know everything, Jack."

It was strange talking to an adult like this, hearing her be so honest and unguarded. It was like seeing your teacher at the grocery store, or watching your parent get a speeding ticket. You realize they're human, after all. Just because someone was a grown-up didn't mean they'd finished growing up.

"Well, you've got quite a friend in Louisa Benning, haven't you?" Belinda said with a smile. "Not many people would do something like that."

"Yeah, not gonna lie, even I was shocked," I confessed. "I've never seen her do anything that crazy before."

Belinda looked at me with the most genuine expression I'd seen since she'd first appeared in our classroom.

"I'm really sorry for how I treated you, Jack."

I gave my shoulders a little shrug, hardly a twitch, but enough to let her know that at least part of me understood.

"Thanks," I said quietly.

Her eyes began gleaming under the auditorium lights, but she jerked her head away and looked around the empty theater.

"So," she said. "What should I do? How do I get everybody back?"

-LOUISA-

This made the second day in a row that I was walking home. Except I wasn't walking, I was running—trying to get away as quickly as I could from that auditorium, from Belinda, from Jack, from my cast, and most of all, from the version of myself that had just screamed at a grown-up and quit the show. In my desperate rush to escape, I had only grabbed my coat, not wanting to spend the extra five seconds it would have taken to dislodge my backpack from underneath one of the seats. This would pose a problem when it came to doing homework later, but homework was the least of my worries right now.

With my arms pumping steadily against the wind, a carousel of images and sounds kept revolving in my head: Belinda's shocked expression, Jack's eyes wide as they pleaded with me to stay quiet, the deafening silence of my castmates after I exploded. I had never, ever done anything like that in my life. And while at the time it felt like there was no way to control what came out of me, now all I thought was: *How could I have done that?*

I was terrified of what I'd left behind—Jack, alone, an even bigger target at whom Belinda could aim her fire; an Adelaide-size hole to be filled by someone who didn't know Jack (or the show) the way I did; an entire team of soccer boys who were all probably laughing about what I'd just done; a backpack full of unfinished assignments . . .

"*Lou!*"

The voice was so faint behind me that I wasn't sure I'd actually heard my name. Still, I slowed to a jog and twisted around to see where the sound was coming from.

About half a block away was Tanner Falzone, running to catch up with me.

"*Hold on!*" he shouted. His long legs helped close

the gap between us fairly quickly, and I noticed as he got closer that he was carrying two backpacks. One of them was mine.

"Jeez, you run pretty fast for a shorty," he said as he reached me, his breath coming out in big clouds of steam.

"What—what are you doing?" I panted.

"Jenny wanted to catch up with you to give you your bag, but she said she couldn't run fast enough in her fried boots."

"Huh?"

"I dunno, something about her fried boots."

I had no idea what Tanner was talking about, but then it struck me that he had simply misheard Jenny's label-dropping.

"*Frye* boots," I said, still breathing heavily. "They're a shoe brand."

"Whatever." Tanner shrugged. "I knew *I* could catch up with you, so I grabbed your bag and started running."

I squinted at him.

"You and Jenny left, too?"

"Everybody did. We all left."

My heart, already beating fast, started to beat even faster.

If everyone had left, did that mean Guys and
Dolls *was officially over?*

I swallowed hard and dared myself to ask
another question, though I dreaded the answer.
"What about Jack?"

Tanner looked back over his shoulder toward
the school as if Jack might suddenly appear in the
distance.

"Uh, actually, I don't know about Jack. I just
know that all the guys left after Jenny, and then
we saw the girls come out when we were still in
the parking lot. I didn't see Jack leave, but . . . it's
not like there was anything left for Belinda to do
once the whole cast was gone."

There were plenty of other things I could
have been thinking about, but the only thought
I had at this moment was that these were by far
the most words I'd ever heard Tanner Falzone
speak. And they were certainly the most he'd ever
spoken to *me*.

I hesitated. I had another question, but I
wasn't sure how long he was planning on treating
me like a real person. Nevertheless, curiosity got
the best of me.

"Why did *you* leave?"

Tanner looked up at the sky, which was getting darker by the minute.

"Um . . . ," he started, "'cause, like, Belinda was being totally harsh. And you know, we all talk about how mean she's been toward Jack, but we just thought that's how it was with real . . . *experienced* kind of actors? Like, how are we supposed to know what's normal? But then, when *you* suddenly got mad, it was like, 'Okay, right. This is uncool.'" He paused, then looked at me in a way that made me feel funny.

"Like, if *you* say she's being unfair, then it's gotta be true. Lou Benning doesn't say stuff she doesn't mean, you know?"

I didn't know what to say. Once again I felt ashamed that I had been so clueless about Belinda's cruelty toward Jack, even while people as seemingly dense as Tanner Falzone were noticing. But there was something else, too, that left me speechless: Tanner Falzone had been *paying attention to me*, not merely dismissing me as some uptight theater nerd. And that made me feel really, really . . . strange. There was an awkward silence between us, and then he thrust my backpack toward me.

"Anyway," he said, "here's your bag."

"Thanks," I said, grabbing one of the straps and tucking it over my shoulder. The cold finally hit me with a freezer-like blast; I started to shiver. I'd forgotten to put on a hat this morning and my ears were not happy. Tanner glanced down at my chattering teeth.

"How far is your house from here?" he asked.

"Like ten more minutes," I said, wondering if I should start running again. I'd get there faster, for sure, but I was also feeling pretty exhausted.

"Well," said Tanner, digging in his coat pocket and producing a knit cap with the Cleveland Browns logo, "take this. You can give it back to me tomorrow."

"Thanks." I put on the cap, and my poor ears felt instant relief. Tanner gave a wry smile.

"It's way big on you."

I couldn't help but smile, too.

"It'll do the trick, though," I said, pulling the other backpack strap over my shoulder. "See you tomorrow."

"Yeah," said Tanner, who surprised me by turning around and heading back in the direction of the school.

"Wait—Tanner!" I blurted out, making him stop and turn back. "Where do *you* live?"

"Oh," he said, a bit sheepishly, "Lyman Boulevard."

"Oh."

His neighborhood was even farther away than mine. Tanner must have seen me drawing a map in my head, because he added hastily, "It's not that far. Remember," he said, nodding toward my legs, "I can run faster than . . ."

"Than me?" I said, rolling my eyes.

"Than anybody," he boasted. "See ya."

And off he went, leaving me to process that Tanner Falzone, class bully, had not only chased me down, returned my bag, paid me a compliment, *and* lent me a hat, but he had also gone *completely out of his way* to do so. I had spent most of grade school avoiding that kid, thinking he was too dopey, too mean, too *unlike me* to bother with. It suddenly occurred to me that in the last twenty-four hours, two people had revealed themselves to be completely different from how I chose to see them. People really could surprise you.

The Cleveland Browns hat was helping, but the rest of my body was begging for warmth; I needed to get home. The Tanner incident had made me feel a little better, but as I hurried to get home, that carousel of faces and voices started spinning, and I was once again reliving the nightmarish scene in the auditorium. What was going to happen now? Would Jack forgive me? What would happen to the soccer team? As Belinda's old friend, would Coach Wilson be forced to punish the boys in some way? Would they be kicked off the team? I felt nauseous as I imagined the disastrous ripple effects of my outburst. And as I got closer to my house, the question that started to burn with the most urgency was: How were my parents going to react to all of this?

"I'm calling Principal Lang first thing in the morning," my mother declared when I finished telling my story. My parents weren't upset with me at all—they were furious with Belinda.

"That woman should know better," my mother continued, angrily stirring a pot of tomato sauce. "Poor Jack! Why didn't he say anything earlier?"

Because he was embarrassed, I thought guiltily, once again recalling how slow I'd been in realizing the full extent of Jack's unhappiness.

"How are *you* feeling, Loulou?" my dad asked, chopping green peppers for a salad. "That must have been pretty scary, standing up to Belinda like that."

"Yeah," I admitted, "it was."

"Brave," said my mom. "It was also brave."

I should have been feeling better. No one had said that I'd done anything wrong; in fact, it seemed like everyone was on my side. Jenny kept sending me text messages, confirming my new reputation of "School Hero":

"OMG u r SO FIERCE!!!"

"KIDS R CALLING U THE DRAGON SLAYER."

But until Jack returned the three voice mails and seven text messages I'd sent him, I couldn't let myself truly believe that I'd done the right thing. I needed to know that Jack had gotten out of that auditorium alive, and that he wasn't mad at me. I kept staring at my phone, waiting for it to light up with his name across the screen. But it didn't. Something else happened instead.

At six thirty, just as Dad was clearing our

dinner plates from the table, our doorbell rang.

"Why don't you answer it, Lou?" Dad said, knowing how badly I wanted Jack to be standing on our front steps.

I forced myself not to run to the door, taking deep breaths and preparing myself for whatever Jack might say to me. But what I wasn't prepared for at all was the sight of both Jack *and* Belinda standing side by side on our stoop.

"Hey, Lou," said Jack, calmly, "is it all right if we come in?"

Belinda looked so out of place in our living room. The soft earth tones of the couch and throw pillows provided a shy, neutral background to Belinda's fiery hair and sparkly shirt. That she looked so uncomfortable only heightened the contrast. My parents stood awkwardly at the bottom of the stairs, uncertain as to their role in the situation. Jack, on the other hand, seemed more relaxed than I'd seen him in weeks. He and I sat across from Belinda in matching armchairs, waiting for someone to speak. Behind us, Dad cleared his throat.

"Um. I think we'll give you guys some privacy."

"Yes," Mom added as she started to follow Dad

up the stairs, "but call us if you need anything."

"I will," I said, turning around to let her see that I was okay. I waited until their footsteps reached the second floor, then turned back to face Belinda.

"So," she finally began, "Jack and I spent the rest of the afternoon . . . clearing the air."

I looked at Jack, who nodded in confirmation.

"And I'd like to . . . apologize to you, Lou, for giving you such a terrible ultimatum earlier. Obviously . . ." Belinda paused. "Obviously that didn't work out for anybody."

She looked at me expectantly, though I wasn't exactly sure what to say.

"I heard everyone left," I said quietly.

"Yes, everyone left." Belinda sighed. "Everyone except for Jack."

I raised my eyebrows at Jack as if to say, *Why?* but he just kept nodding, waiting for Belinda to continue.

"I'm sure Jack will fill you in on our conversation, and I hope he does—because I want you *both* to understand why I've been behaving in such a way."

Only hours ago we'd all been engaged in battle, with no clear end in sight. But now here sat

Belinda, in complete surrender, and she seemed like a different person.

"While I am here to apologize," she went on, "I am also here to ask for your help."

Jack tucked a leg underneath him and leaned toward me. "You have to get the cast to come back," he said earnestly.

"Please," implored Belinda, "since you're the one they followed out of that auditorium, it means you're the one they'll follow back in."

They were both completely serious. I was dying to know what Belinda had said to Jack that had made him this committed to keeping the show alive. But I'd just have to wait to find out until after she'd left. In the meantime, they needed an answer.

"Okay, but . . . I'm not the only one they'll follow," I said slowly, fixing my eyes on Jack. "They'll follow both of us. We can work together to bring everybody back."

"Thank you." Belinda exhaled with relief. "I'm really sorry. I know I've been a lot to take." She shifted on the couch, measuring her words carefully.

"It's funny—I was about to say that it's only because this show means a great deal to me, but the truth is—this show means a great deal to all of us." Belinda looked at me and Jack, her eyes now glistening.

"You two aren't on that stage just for yourselves, the way I used to be. I am truly impressed—and inspired—by how much you care about each other."

Belinda rose from the couch, gathered her coat, and headed toward the door, but not before stopping to place a hand on each of our heads.

"You've both taught me something today."

And moments later, she was out the door and turning the key in her car's ignition, leaving Jack and me alone.

"So," I said, "you're not mad at me?"

Jack smiled and shook his head.

"No. I thought you lost your mind, but I was never mad. I couldn't believe it when I looked up and saw you marching off the stage. That took some guts, Lou."

I wondered how long people at school would be talking about me. I wondered if Tanner would be talking about me, and I suddenly experienced the same funny feeling I'd had when he'd looked at me.

"Are you okay?" Jack asked, startling me out of my thoughts and making my cheeks go red.

"Oh yeah," I said, covering, "I was just thinking

that I couldn't stay there and let Belinda talk to you like that."

"Yeah, no one could," Jack snorted, "not even Tanner Falzone."

"I know, he—" I began, then stopped myself as I felt my cheeks burning. Again.

"What?" Jack said, his eyes widening, "Tanner what?"

"I'll tell you in a sec," I said, trying to sound casual. "First tell me what Belinda said to you."

Jack eyed me with suspicion.

"All right, then I'll go fast, because I *need* to know what you're talking about."

"Wait," I said, hopping up from my chair, "let me get some chips for this. I barely ate dinner."

"Yeah, good call—I haven't eaten at all. Is it okay if I take off my shoes?"

"Totally!"

It was a cold winter night, but my house was cozy and warm. There was an unopened bag of potato chips in the pantry and a Cleveland Browns knit cap shoved in the sleeve of my parka. Best of all, my friend Jack Goodrich was waiting in the living room to tell me a story, and no dragon was going to get in the way of that.

-JACK-

Our first day back in rehearsal was like walking into an audition waiting room. Except this time it wasn't the students who were auditioning. Belinda paced nervously across the stage, waiting for our cast to file in. Her eyes were fixed on the double doors, watching to see if everyone would return.

I already knew she didn't have anything to worry about. As soon as Lou told me about her run-in with Tanner, it was clear he'd do anything she asked.

"Ohmigosh, he totally likes you!" I said that evening in her living room.

"He does not!" she cried back.

"Whatever, we are *totally* going to milk this for all it's worth."

I ducked as Lou hurled a chip at me, her face turning bright red.

Once Belinda apologized, she wasted no time in getting us back to work. Our cast began filing up the stairs to the stage, but before Jenny would leave her seat, she turned to us.

"Are you sure this is okay? 'Cause I do *not* want to waste a fan kick on her."

"Trust us!" Lou said.

Belinda was back! With rehearsals once again under way, the show did a complete one-eighty. Belinda now approached our production with an air of collaboration. When we got to the scene in Act 2 where the gamblers take to the sewers to shoot dice, we waited for her to come up and set the blocking that had been used on Broadway.

"You know, why don't you try doing the scene once by yourselves?" Belinda said, looking up from her script.

"I'd be interested to see what comes up *organically*," she said, almost shuddering at the word.

The result was hilarious. Especially when we got to the part where Big Jule threatens Nathan for refusing to join the game.

"*Why not?!*" Tanner said threateningly, grabbing on to the collar of my shirt. Instinctively, I wrapped my hands around his wrists, and he was able to lift me off the floor, my legs kicking as I squeaked out my line.

"*I see no reason.*"

For the first time in weeks, Belinda made the sound I'd been dying to hear—laughter.

"Did you guys plan that beforehand?" she asked, giggling at the conclusion of the scene.

"No," Tanner replied, turning to me. "And for a little guy, you're heavier than you look."

Everyone burst out laughing.

"Maybe you're just weaker than you thought," Sebastian teased.

With Belinda's blessing, our cast felt like they had permission to play, to see what came naturally, rather than using what had worked on Broadway twenty years ago. By the time we got to our final dress rehearsal, we'd created a show that everyone could be proud of. While Belinda still served as our leader, there wasn't a single cast member who didn't make their mark in some way.

Opening nights always held a little bit of magic—the dressing rooms with fresh flowers, the nervous excitement sweeping through the halls like a force field, and the understanding that no matter how many things went wrong in the dress rehearsal, we would somehow get through it as a cast.

Over in the girls' dressing room, Lou was perched in front of her mirror. Belinda stood close behind, armed with a curling iron.

"So the pieces in the front," she said, wrapping a strand of Lou's hair around the hot iron, "you want to curl them in the direction *away* from your face."

Who knew Belinda was also a master when it came to hair and makeup tricks?

"That's how you get that Broadway showgirl look."

A cluster of girls looked on, wrapping their bangs around two of their fingers in imitation.

"And once you put on your final coat of lipstick," she said, shifting over to Bridget's dressing station, "use an eye-shadow brush to dust your lips with a little bit of blush. That way it won't get on your costumes when you're doing a quick change."

Even Jenny, a self-proclaimed makeup expert, couldn't help eavesdropping, reaching stealthily for her own makeup brush.

Choosing my favorite moment of *Guys and Dolls* would be almost impossible. We made so many memories on opening night alone, like when Lou and I performed "Sue Me." How we made ourselves red in the face holding out the *"All riiiiiiiiiiiight already"* to a comically long length, each daring each other to be the first to cut off.

Or maybe it was the scene where Sky confesses his real name, Obediah, to Sarah Brown after sharing their first kiss. Since day one, Sebastian and Bridget had been nervous about it, and after a few awkward attempts in rehearsal, they both agreed that Sebastian should just place a thumb between their mouths before turning upstage and fake smooching. But on closing night, with apparently nothing to lose, shy little Bridget Livak grabbed him by the face and planted one on him like a starlet in a Hollywood romance film. Dumbfounded, Sebastian just stared at her, totally blanking on his next line. Finally Bridget just reached into his pocket and pulled out his prop wallet, pretending to find a driver's license and gasping in feigned surprise. *"Obediah, what kind of a name is that?!"*

Or perhaps it was getting to perform "Sit Down, You're Rockin' the Boat," how impossible those tricky harmonies seemed that first day and how polished they sounded now, even earning a standing ovation at the closing performance. Or maybe it was the first time we made it through the "Crapshooters' Dance," how Tanner's words of "can't" and "dance" still rang in my ears from the audition. It was so cool to watch the boys prove to the whole school that just because you're a boy doesn't mean you can't dance.

The thing I couldn't get used to was saying good-bye to a show after only three performances. *Into the Woods* had been the same way. Three performances felt like nothing! On Broadway, three shows passed in the blink of an eye, yet here we were, dropping the curtain on the musical we'd rehearsed for two months. As we took our final bow, I looked around in disbelief as I thought of our costumes that would be packed up and the sets that would be broken down. The orchestra played its final chords, sending us rushing backstage to change into our party clothes. While I was excited to celebrate the success of the run, there was still something I wanted to do, so as my castmates dashed out to hug their families, I hung back, hoping to get one last look.

The auditorium was silent. It had a kind of musty warmth, like the smell of old clothes you'd forgotten about, buried in a box in the back of your closet. Even though the room was empty, it still buzzed, a reminder of the magic that had just happened within its walls. The cheering parents and friends had made their way out to the lobby, leaving me alone onstage, at least for a few minutes before our custodian would emerge to sweep up the abandoned programs and fallen candy wrappers. I loved standing onstage after a performance. Even after years of performing, often in much bigger houses, looking out into a vacant theater still gave me a rush. It seemed so full of possibilities. Looking down at my feet, I thought about all the things that had happened in this very spot.

Hearing footsteps, I turned to find Lou, still in her period hairstyle, carrying her makeup box and dance bag.

"Congrats, buddy! You were SO great," she said in a cartoony voice. "Remember when you had to practice saying that in New York? *You were SOOO great.*"

"Ugh. Don't remind me," I groaned, cringing at the memory.

"Can you believe that was only a few months ago?"

It was true. The Ohio snow had only just melted, but with all that had happened with *Guys and Dolls*, New York felt like ages ago.

"I'm just teasing." She grinned, joining me at the edge of the stage. "And I actually do mean it. You *were* so great."

"Thanks, Lou," I replied. "So were you. I really lucked out."

Hearing these words were nice, but they did make me think of that backstage meeting with Corey and the praise I never gave him. It was

probably time to shoot him an email and send
that long overdue congratulations. After all that
had happened with Belinda, I realized that if you
couldn't help feeling jealous, you could at least
control the way it affected others.

I reached up and straightened my fedora
(as a show of solidarity, all the boys decided we
were going to wear our hats to the cast party). I
wondered how ridiculous we must have looked—
old-timey looks on top, cast T-shirts and jeans on
the bottom.

"Do you need a ride over to Geraci's Restaurant
for the cast party?" Lou asked.

"No," I responded, "my parents and Nana came
again tonight, so I'll just head over with them."

"Well, well, well," a voice called from behind us.
"If it isn't my little guy and doll."

"Hey, Belinda," we said, turning to find her
striking a pose. She was wearing shiny black
high-waisted pants, red suspenders, and a ruffled
tuxedo-style shirt and a bow tie. She looked ready
to perform some modern tango number on *So You
Think You Can Dance*.

"Shouldn't you guys be stuffing your faces with
pizza right now?" she asked.

"Probably." Lou shrugged. "We were just getting ready to leave."

"It was a good show tonight, wasn't it?" Belinda said, slinking downstage.

"It really was," we chimed in unison.

"I thought the scene at the Hot Box Club was the best it's ever been," she said, sidling up to us. "I'm so glad you guys thought up that bit with the wedding veil. It *slayed* tonight."

"Aw, thanks," we said together.

"So what are you going to do now that the show is over?" I asked Belinda somewhat warily.

"Obviously you have to stay forever," Lou insisted.

"Well, funny you should say that," Belinda said, crossing her arms. "I just spoke with Principal Lang tonight—*who went bananas for the show, by the way*—and it sounds like Mrs. Wagner is recovering well, so she'll be more than ready to return in the fall."

We nodded, trying not to look disappointed, out of respect for the poor woman.

"But . . . ," she continued, a coy smile curling the edges of her mouth. "She's decided to just stick with teaching music, so it looks like I'll be staying on to direct your next musical."

Lou let out a shriek of excitement as my face broke out in an enormous grin.

"That means I'll need you to put on your thinking caps and help me come up with a show that would be fun to do. Think you can do that?" She winked.

I couldn't help myself; I lunged in and hugged Belinda around the waist. Lou joined me, flinging her arms over mine. Belinda said nothing, just held our shoulders as we hugged her tightly.

After a moment, Lou spoke up, her face still squished against my arm. "*Thoroughly Modern Millie.*"

"Ohh, so you can play Millie," I said, rolling my eyes, still clinging to Belinda. "No, let's do something edgy, like *Caroline, or Change.*"

"Are you crazy?" Lou pinched me. "We're in middle school," she whined. "But . . . if you happened to choose *Cabaret*, I know someone who'd be a great Sally Bowles."

"Hey, you can't just pick shows that you'd be the star of," I grunted. "How about *A Catered Affair*?"

"*Evita.*"

"*Dogfight.*"

"*Wicked.*"

"Natasha, Pierre and the Great Comet of 1812."

"Well, looks like you've got your work cut out for you," Belinda said, gently prying us off of her. "We should probably get to that cast party."

I nodded, remembering that our parents were still waiting patiently in the lobby.

"I have to run backstage and grab all my flowers. I'll see you guys over there," Belinda said, giving our shoulders a little squeeze before strutting back into the wings. I looked over at Lou, grinning as we walked to the staircase.

"Our carriage awaits," I said, holding out my hand like a coachman.

"Well, ain'tchyoo a gent!" Lou responded in her Adelaide voice.

She placed her hand on top of mine, and we waltzed down the stairs together. We strolled up the aisle, giggling as we shouted out more and more ridiculous musicals we could do next year. Our feet glided past rows of empty chairs, seats that would stay vacant for a while but would be filled next year, when we'd get to do it all over again.

Guys and Dolls is a classic American musical comedy with music and lyrics by Frank Loesser and book by Jo Swerling and Abe Burrows. It premiered on Broadway at the 46th Street Theatre on November 24, 1950. It won several Tony Awards, including Best Musical and Best Director (George S. Kaufman). The original production ran for 1,200 performances. Five years later, an MGM film adaptation starring Frank Sinatra and Marlon Brando opened to wide acclaim.

Since its original production, *Guys and Dolls* has been remounted several times in the United States and internationally. The most successful American revival was the iconic 1992 Broadway production starring Nathan Lane as Nathan Detroit, Peter Gallagher as Sky Masterson, Faith Prince as Miss Adelaide, and Josie de Guzman as Sarah Brown.

ACKNOWLEDGMENTS

Jack and Louisa's journey remains supported and uplifted by some amazing people: Francesco Sedita, Sarah Fabiny, and Max Bisantz at Penguin; Chris and Arnold Wetherhead, Jeff Croiter, Scott Bixby, Jake Wilson, Benj Pasek, and David Hull. Once again, Ben Fankhauser graciously offered his knowledge of Shaker Heights. We are eternally grateful to the astoundingly talented community of New York artists, many of whom we are lucky enough to call our friends, and from whom we draw daily inspiration. As always, the theaters of our past provide incredible memories that we have enjoyed exaggerating, distorting, and celebrating in order to create Jack and Louisa's world. Lastly, thank you to our fans who have reached out to us to share their personal MTN stories. These books are for you.